Murder
at
Fantasia Fair

A Provincetown Mystery

Jeannette de Beauvoir

best wishes,
Jeannette

HOMEPORT
P R E S S

Murder At Fantasia Fair: A Provincetown Mystery
Copyright © 2017 by Jeannette de Beauvoir

Published by HomePort Press
PO Box 1508
Provincetown, MA 02657
www.HomePortPress.com

ISBN   978-0-9992451-2-5
eISBN 978-0-9992451-1-8

Cover Design by Miladinka Milic

Other Books
by
Jeannette de Beauvoir

Mysteries:
In Dark Woods
The Provincetown Theme Week mysteries:
     Death of a Bear
The Martine LeDuc series:
     Deadly Jewels
     Asylum
The Trinity Pierce series:
     Murder Most Academic (as Alicia Stone)

Historical Fiction:
Our Lady of the Dunes
The Crown & The Kingdom

1

It was the gunshot that woke me.

I didn't know that it was a gunshot, of course, just that I was suddenly sitting bolt upright in bed, my heart pounding. *Breathe, Riley, just breathe*, I told myself. Easier said than done when you're suddenly scared out of your wits and you don't know why.

Scared out of what little wits I had left, that is.

I snapped on the bedside light. Ibsen was blinking and looking at me reproachfully; whatever the noise was, it wasn't in his portfolio of Things That Cats Should Be Scared Of.

Maybe I'd imagined it, after all.

I got up and went into my kitchen (the size of my apartment, this wasn't a stretch), poured myself a glass of water, listened to the world outside. There wasn't anything happening that I could perceive as untoward, so I got back in bed. My imagination is often to blame for problems in my life. I am Anxiety Girl, from zero to panic in half a second or less.

Back in bed, sleep eluded me. Ibsen settled himself more comfortably after the outrage of being awakened and began to snore softly. I hate it when I can't sleep. I feel that I ought to be using the time productively, somehow, but I'm too tired to do anything but try to sleep. Which, of course, is the one thing I can't do. Circular stuff for sure.

There was plenty to be worried about. I'm the wedding coordinator at Race Point Inn in Provincetown, which generally *guarantees* a lot of worry, but the wedding season was nearing a close—it was October, after all— and usually this is the time that I, like the rest of the town, am able to slow down and breathe again. But this year was different, as Glenn, the inn's owner, had volunteered us to host P'town's weeklong yearly celebration known as Fantasia Fair.

It didn't mean more weddings, but it was definitely an all-hands-on-deck sort of situation, and so I was helping out. None of us had ever had much to do with the Fair before, and the learning curve was steep.

Glenn had thought from the start that it would be a great idea to have one of the town's theme weeks headquartered at Race Point Inn. Since his late partner—and my late boss—had been killed the year before, Glenn was taking us in different directions from Barry's vision for the inn. Whereas Barry had been looking to physically enlarge the Race Point, Glenn wanted to plunge it deeper into the town's activities instead. We'd hosted a small art retreat last fall, the first autumn since Barry's death, and now we were moving up with the Fantasia Fair people.

I sighed, pushed back my duvet, and got up. This was ridiculous. Why didn't I ever have sleeping pills in the house? And what was that sound I'd heard? I curled up on the sofa and turned on a reading light. Fantasia Fair started tomorrow. Maybe I was just nervous. Maybe that's all it was.

I opened my laptop and reviewed what was going on. Fantasia Fair comprises a week of workshops, festivities, and social networking for trans people at all points along the spectrum, from those who cross-dress once a year to those who've had the surgery to change their original physical gender…and everyone in between. Mostly it's men—straight men—who celebrate their feminine side more than most.

My boyfriend, Ali, who lives in Boston and so isn't part of Provincetown's day-to-day pageantry, had a tough time understanding it all. "So it's guys who dress in drag," he said. "You have a *week* for that?"

"It's not drag," I said, though in some cases it did rather look something like that. "Drag is a *parody* of women. Drag exaggerates all the things that are part of a male vision of women: high heels, makeup, sexualized clothing, all that. It's buying into some female stereotype that was created by men." I saw I'd lost him and tried again. "Okay, so some gay men dress in glitzy women's clothing for a drag show. For entertainment purposes." There were certainly enough of *those* in town in the summer months; the Silly Season is filled with shows: Miss Richfield, Scarbie, Anita Cocktail, Varla Jean, Dina Martina. "But then there are men who want to be women, who maybe have always felt they were supposed to have been born women, and they dress as women to feel comfortable."

He just kept looking at me. I'm clearly not the world's best explainer. But in my defense, it's not an easy topic. Once Glenn decided a year ago that we'd host the event, I started seriously trying to understand something I'd been only peripherally aware of in the past, and all I came up with was layers and layers of questions. The relationship of trans women to women who were born women. How to stop the horrific amount of violence against trans people. How to *refer* to trans people, even. What changed in relationships when people went through the transition from one gender to another.

I sighed and closed the laptop. Questions that could keep the most hardened of philosophers sleepless for months; I wasn't going to solve any of them tonight.

***

As usual, it was my friend Mirela who had all the latest and greatest.

Mirela is from Bulgaria. She's an artist who came here to do menial summer jobs and now her paintings start somewhere around five thousand dollars. She's also the queen of gossip (and this in a town filled with gossipy old ladies, most of whom are men), and anytime I need to get the lowdown, I go to her.

"Someone shot themselves last night," she told me on the telephone before breakfast.

I was trying to hold my smartphone between my ear and my shoulder while I opened a can of food for Ibsen, no easy feat. I miss that about old telephones: you could just jam the receiver there and chat for hours. "What? Who?"

"I think it is whom," she said primly. Mirela speaks about five languages, all of them better than most Americans speak English.

"I don't care," I said. "Who shot themselves?"

"It was an argument," she said, then, apparently invigorated, warmed to her subject. "Oh, sunshine, it is so tragic. They were supposed to love each other forever and always, and then *pouf*! You bring in alcohol and drugs and before you know it, everything goes to hell." I think that in Bulgarian "sunshine" is a straightforward term of endearment. When I hear it, all I can think of is a line from *One Night in Bangkok*.

"No one usually brings in *guns*," I said cautiously. Massachusetts has one of the strictest firearms laws in the country. "Who was it, Mirela?"

"People not from here," she said dismissively. If Mirela can't get good gossip out of something, she loses interest. "Besides, they couldn't aim, they missed. They didn't even go to the hospital. Tourists."

October's a little late in the year for tourists. Provincetown hosts a wide range of theme weeks throughout the summer season, and October—with Fantasia Fair and Women's Week—is pretty much the last hurrah. The same people who crowd the beaches and the clubs in the summer don't feel quite so enamored of the place when November's cold winds blow in off the Atlantic. "Oh, God," I said, as a terrible thought occurred to me. "It's nothing to do with Fantasia Fair, is it?" It had been a bad year in America for trans people, with a murder rate that would make Idi Amin blush, but Provincetown's supposed to be *safe*…

"Not at all," she said. "Marc told me that it's just finance people from Boston."

Well, that was something, anyway.

***

The inn looked fantastic: I had to give Glenn that. Well, it had always looked fantastic, but there was a certain gaiety about the place today that had me humming the moment I got in. Rachel Parsons, the coordinator for Fantasia Fair, was standing beside the front desk, calmly ticking off items on a clipboard. I tapped her on the shoulder. "Hey, Rachel."

She glanced at me. "Good morning, Sydney," she said. "You look awful."

"Thanks ever so much," I said sourly. "Couldn't sleep."

"They make pills for that sort of thing nowadays," she observed, her eyes back on her paperwork.

"None that are available at three in the morning."

She glanced at me, amused. "You should live in New York City," she said. "There's nothing that you can't get at three in the morning there."

"Thanks, but no thanks." Provincetown's just the right size for me. In the winter I can go to the Stop & Shop and recognize everybody I see there. In the summer the town is flooded with visitors; and, in some way or another, most of us who live here year-round make our livings catering to those visitors. Sometimes I think it's the contrast between the two seasons that's most appealing. "Anyway, my cat would have kept me awake even with pills. He snores."

"Cats snore?" She stared at me, momentarily distracted. "Who knew?"

"Stick with me. I'll fill your head with all sorts of useless facts." I slid past the counter to the space where I worked, tucked aside from the day-to-day business of the inn: a roll top desk, a very big calendar, and a wastepaper basket. My domain, such as it was. "Anyone arrive yet?"

"Heavens, yes," Rachel said. "The meet-and-greet isn't until six o'clock tonight, it always is, but that's never stopped people from getting here early, and already there are about a million questions."

I sat down and opened my laptop. "You must be used to it," I said.

She sighed. "Yes, I suppose I must."

I looked up at her. Rachel is tall—well, many trans women are, having begun life as males—and seemed even taller from where I was sitting. "You suppose you must? That doesn't sound so positive. Isn't that your *job*?"

"Of course it is. But sometimes I feel like, gosh, maybe they can just look at the schedule I hand them, or even go all-out and Google something for themselves. How far to the Monument?" She rolled her eyes.

"How far is it? You can *see* the frigging Monument from here."

"Ah, that kind of question," I said, nodding sagely. "Welcome to my world." I grinned. "Last week, someone asked me what we do with the Monument in the winter. I wanted to say that we roll it up and put it in storage."

Rachel laughed. "Tourists. Gotta love them."

"Well, that, or starve," I said cheerfully.

She turned as someone came through the door: an African-American man in khakis and a t-shirt and a large garment bag over his shoulder. "Bruce! Good to see you again!" They air-kissed each other's cheeks. Rachel glanced at me. "Is there someone to check him in?"

I sighed and got up. We'd once had an absolutely fabulous front desk maven, but after he left there wasn't anyone who had his work ethic. Patrick, who was supposed to be there now, was—well, obviously, elsewhere. I gave Bruce a bright smile. "I can do it," I said. "You have a reservation?"

He nodded. "Patterson."

I pulled it up on the computer. "Six nights," I read aloud. "Do you have the card you charged it to?" No wonder Patrick had disappeared. No one works the front desk of

10

a hotel for the joy of the repetitive tasks the job involves; but there were other perks. The Race Point Inn is one of the largest in town, with a swimming pool, an events patio (where I organize a lot of weddings), two dining areas and an award-winning restaurant, a spa… I could go on and on (and frequently do), but the point is that employees get to use all of those amenities. The inn's open year-round, too, which makes for more regular employment than what's generally offered in a town as seasonal as ours. So with all those incentives, why wasn't Patrick at his post doing the rote parts of checking guests in?

Bruce headed up to his room and Rachel made a note. "Last time you'll see him," she said.

"Why?" I looked at her, startled. "He spends the week in his room?"

"He spends the week as Lisa," she said. "Look, Sydney, people like Bruce, they can't be themselves anywhere but here. He has a high security-clearance job, he's a deacon in his Evangelical-leaning church, and if he ever let Lisa come out at home he'd lose everything."

"You know a lot about him."

"I know a lot about most of the fair's participants," she said simply. "Lisa's been coming for years." She caught my look. "What?"

"It just seems so sad," I said, realizing as I spoke how inadequate my words were. "Only being able to be yourself for one week out of the year."

"Yes," she said. "And welcome to *my* world."

2

Ali had the week off, an event almost un-heard of in our experience thus far as a cou-ple. He worked for US Immigration and Customs Enforcement, the dreaded ICE, which typically would have put us on oppo-site sides of any fence, but a year ago, when we first met, he'd transferred to the section dealing with human trafficking. It wasn't go-ing to last forever—burnout was rampant—but he was a lot happier doing that than what he'd been doing before. On the flip side, his hours were horrific, and a week together seemed beyond luxurious.

And then on the flip side of *that*, we hadn't known the inn was going to be hosting Fantasia Fair back when he'd requested the time off.

"Are you sure you still want me to come down?" he'd asked on the phone. He had nearly two summers with me under his belt already and knew how insane it could be when I was working. Or maybe just how insane *I* could be.

"No, no, you should come. I'm really only helping out. And P'town's nice in the fall."

He arrived not long after Bruce-who-we-wouldn't-see-again, walking into reception with the sun behind him. The first time I'd met Ali was here at the inn, back when he'd arrived to interrogate my extremely recently deceased boss. I'd liked his looks right away, which was singularly unfortunate (I did mention ICE, didn't I?), and now he still had the ability to catch and hold my attention, even once he'd learned that most guys in town don't wear suits. The suit may make the man; Ali, in my opinion, made the suit.

Today he was wearing jeans and a chamois shirt. Dark hair, dark eyes, really *nice* dark eyes… "Am I interrupting?"

I kissed him. "Checking people in," I said, "since Patrick has apparently checked himself *out*. Ali, this is Rachel Parsons; Rachel, Ali

Hakim." They were about the same height, but Rachel was cheating; she was wearing heels. "Well," she said, correctly intercepting the look between us, "I'm going to get some coffee and figure out how to introduce the workshop speakers."

"You're very discreet," I told her.

"An asset *you'd* better have, here at the front desk."

Ali watched her go. "So she's…"

"A trans woman," I said.

"Because she's had surgery?" Ali's Muslim; his parents are both from Lebanon. This was pretty much outside any experience or knowledge he'd ever had. I had to give him points for wanting to understand.

"I don't know if she has or not," I confessed. "It–um–hasn't come up." And unlike a singularly unfortunate TV interview I'd seen featuring newscaster Katie Couric, I wasn't about to ask anybody about their genitalia.

I'd only met Rachel at the beginning of the summer, when she'd arrived for long meetings with Glenn and Mike, the inn's manager, and I'd been called in to help. We weren't quite that close. I don't know how close you have to be to talk about your sex organs, but I was perfectly fine never knowing. Just not my business. "But it doesn't matter. I mean, it's important to respect people, no matter where they are on the spectrum."

"The spectrum," he repeated. "Maybe I need a coffee too."

I laughed. "It's easy. One end totally male. The other end totally female. Some people need to be at one end or the other, and some people are comfortable with spaces in between: maybe you only dress like your female self once a year, or maybe you get to dress like her a lot, or maybe you've been taking hormones to become her more completely, or maybe–"

He held up his hand. "A little complicated for me," he said. He really didn't have anything in his past to which he could compare this. And it was probably all moving a little too fast for him. I had to remember that prior to last year he hadn't had much exposure to anyone who wasn't heterosexual.

"I just checked someone in who will be a woman all week," I said, slowly, thinking about it, "and then who'll go back to his life as a man for the next fifty-one weeks. I think that's inexpressibly sad. That he can't be himself–herself–all the time." I shivered. "You know, people like us, we're lucky."

He looked puzzled. "Because we're straight?"

"No." I shook my head. "Because we can live out who we are and not have to pay a price for it."

***

There's something exciting about the start to any theme week: a sense of expectation, of possibilities, of joy. People come to our little seaside town for a lot of reasons, but the theme weeks are especially poignant, I've always felt. They might have been originally intended as marketing ploys (what isn't, these days?) but quickly slipped into something special and treasured and–dare I say it–holy. They provide a lot of things, but mainly it's a chance to connect with other people who are like you.

Back in the bad old days when it was illegal to be gay, Provincetown was one of the few places where you could walk down the street holding your partner's hand—and yes, the desire really was that simple. To not have to hide, be it for an hour, a day, a week. To be able to be yourself.

Things were easing off in that respect, at least in parts of the United States; there were a lot of places now where being gay was tolerated and even occasionally celebrated, and the country as a whole even allowed you to actually marry your partner, what a thought. Slow progress, unforgivably slow, but progress all the same.

But I was coming to the understanding that the trans community hadn't been as fortunate as the other letters in the LGBTQ acronym. There was a definite unevenness in the world's acceptance, or lack thereof. Hate crimes against trans people were on the rise, not on the decline. It was a big bad world out there, and coming here, even for just a week, had to feel like entering another world, walking on enchanted ground. Maybe that's why I could feel a humming of excitement, something intensely electric and energetic and celebratory in the air.

Mike arrived mid-morning, "Hey, Sydney."

I glanced up from the reception computer. "Who are you?" I asked. "It's not Monday."

"I know." Mike isn't usually at work on a weekend, but he always comes in to help out with problems whenever he's needed. Maybe, in this case, to forestall problems before they began. I didn't see any problems yet, aside from The Mystery of The Disappearing Front Desk Clerk. But then again, we really didn't quite know how to host this event, and we were all was determined to make a success of it. "And you're not Patrick," he observed.

"Patrick," I said without a shred of loyalty, "is MIA. But not to worry. Sydney Riley, wedding coordinator and general factotum, at your service. We aim to please."

"Glad someone around here does," growled Mike in a way that boded ill for the unfortunate Patrick. "How's it going?"

"Rachel's doing most of the work," I confessed. The martyr thing could only work for so long anyway. "She's getting people organized and oriented. Most of them don't seem to need it; it's just the new venue that's changed for them. They've been coming to Fantasia Fair for years."

"I need coffee," he said. Even midmorning on a Sunday could feel very early, I suppose. I felt no sympathy; I hadn't exactly gotten my full eight hours in, either. "Ali's in there," I said, indicating the dining room with my head. For reasons that I may never understand, and despite being completely different from each other in every possible way except for the obvious one, Mike and Ali really hit it off. They were friends on Facebook. They emailed each other articles and memes. They kayaked together when Ali was in town.

Well, I should amend that: they hit it off once they got the whole ICE investigation from last year out of the way. That had been a little tricky.

"Patrick had better not be there, too," Mike said darkly and headed in the direction of coffee and conversation. And I looked up cheerfully to check the next group of people in. There was, I decided, nothing to this.

By noontime Patrick had been fired and the lobby was starting to fill with very statuesque, very well-dressed trans women. They don't necessarily go in for the whole glamour routine; actually, a couple of them reminded me of my friend Vernon, who as his alternate persona Lady Di pretty much dresses like someone's grandmother. Complete with cat-eye glasses.

Most of them smiled at me cheerfully and then were off, sometimes as couples, sometimes in chattering groups. They didn't need to ask where to go for lunch; they already had favorite haunts they were anxious to revisit. Ali was sitting at my desk behind me, surfing the Net. "So," he inquired, "how long exactly are you on front desk duty?"

"Until Brian comes in at three," I said. "I'm sorry, I didn't mean to be quite so tied down."

He raised his eyebrows. "Ignoring the salacious verbal opening she gave him, he behaves himself and offers instead to fetch her a sandwich for lunch," he said.

I smiled; I couldn't help it. "I'd love one."

"Great." He stood up and stretched. "After that I think I'll go up to the Monument," he said. Ali had developed a puzzling relationship with the Pilgrim Monument, the tall tower that overlooks P'town and commemorates the little-known fact that the Pilgrims spent their first months here before shoving off for Plymouth and its famous rock. The Mayflower Compact was written in Provincetown Harbor; who knew? Besides the Monument, there's a museum up on the hill, a small café, and a lot of lawn with—it has to be said—breathtaking views of Cape Cod Bay. I had no idea what he did when he was up there.

The sandwich was inspired; our diva chef Adrienne doesn't work the lunch shift, but her recipes do. About half an hour after Ali left, a group of three women—clearly *biological* women—came to check in. I dithered at the computer, trying to match each of them up to–what? a husband? What was the right thing to say?

Rachel swooped in and rescued me. "Ladies, I want you to meet Sydney Riley," she said. "She's an absolute angel and this is her first time at Fantasia Fair."

"It's my first time, too," said one of them, a dark-haired petite woman I guessed to be around my own age. She smiled at me, but even on a few hours' sleep I could recognize the nervousness behind the smile. I put out my hand to shake hers. "Sydney," I said.

She smiled, a little less timidly. "Elizabeth."

"Great, welcome!" Rachel said, "and this is Taisie Murray and Megan Hamilton," she said. "I think their significant others already arrived." I loved Rachel for that: answering my unspoken question without making me show my ignorance. I smiled at her warmly.

Megan laughed. "Are you kidding? Sherry's been packed for a week. I think she was the first one to get here."

Elizabeth wasn't playing, though. "Um–Robert–Bob–my husband–he's actually not here yet. It's our–um–first time. He wanted–he wanted to go shopping first. But he didn't know how, or where." She looked completely lost.

Taisie put out a hand and touched the other woman's arm. "We've all been there," she said gently. "I'm sure that there will be something in town. And if not, there are plenty of people here who could help out."

Rachel nodded. "There's a fair bit of clothing exchanges every year," she said. "Robert can always borrow something. And speaking of Robert: does he–is there another name to use this week?" And how careful, I thought, everyone was in the way they talked around their pronouns. The young people, Rachel had told me, wanted to institute "they" in place of every pronoun; "but it's awkward," she said. "Language isn't really our friend here. It follows social change; it doesn't create it."

It was an interesting thought; I filed it away for sometime when I had a spare moment to consider the question. That moment was certainly showing no signs of arriving anytime soon. "Name?" I asked.

Elizabeth blushed. "Robert Gonzalez," she said. "Robert and Elizabeth Gonzalez." She cleared her throat. "He–um–wants to be called Angela."

"Then Angela it is," said Rachel heartily, writing it down. I'd never be able to do what she does. She looked up from the clipboard. "Hey, I have an idea! Why don't you ladies go up to your rooms, unpack, whatever, and then come down and join me and Sydney for a glass of wine?"

I glared at her; it wasn't yet one o'clock. She met my eyes over the women's heads and

I read something there. Not pleading, exactly, but a question. And part of my job is to be an ambassador; she was reminding me of something I already knew. *You want to know about us?* the look asked. *Here's a place to start.* "Sure," I said. "I'll get someone to cover the desk. Why not be a little decadent, after all?"

"Really?" Taisie seemed pleased. She actually giggled. "What fun! We'll get you totally in the know, and we can help Elizabeth pick out workshops for the week!"

Elizabeth looked like she'd just as soon have a root canal, but the third woman—Megan—took her arm. "It'll be good for you to have us around," she said gently. "Your experience here is going to be way different from Angela's. We can help with that."

"Angela," echoed Elizabeth, her voice flat. She took a deep breath, and straightened her shoulders. "Yes," she said. "I'd like that."

But I wondered, as I watched them go toward the stairs, just how much she was going to like any part of this week.

3

We didn't sit in the main bar, which was rapidly filling up with meet-and-greeters, but in what Mike likes to refer to as the "parlor," a smallish room with sofas and chairs and a TV set, should guests not want to watch in their rooms, or want a little privacy without going upstairs. I'd grabbed a bottle of Côtes du Rhône and another of chilled Sancerre (despite Martin the maître-d' frowning his displeasure) and it seemed cozy enough.

Elizabeth looked like she needed a bottle all to herself.

"I appreciate you taking the time," Rachel was saying to them as I opened the bottles with a lot less panache than Martin would have shown. "Sydney here is completely new to the scene."

Thus prompted, I nodded. "And I don't want to make a faux pas," I said. "I've always known about Fantasia Fair, of course, but I'm ashamed to say that after years of living in P'town, all this is still uncharted territory for me."

Megan laughed. "Uncharted for everyone," she said, accepting a glass from me. "The thing is, we're really just making it up as we go along. All of us. And it's constantly changing, too. For the young kids, something like Fantasia Fair isn't even necessary anymore."

"Shut your mouth," said Rachel, mocking-reprovingly.

"But it's true! They don't come here, everyone for them us like, well, duh, so what? It's a non-issue. No one cares. It's all very healthy."

"We still need you, Rachel, don't worry," said Taisie with a smile. Rachel made a face and grinned.

Megan said, "And our lives change a lot, too. If you could have told me when I first met Jeff that I'd end up being in love with someone called Sherry…"

"Sounds like coming out," said Taisie. "As a lesbian, I mean."

"But that's what I am," said Megan, then stopped herself. "Sort of," she amended. "It's odd, in a sense, isn't it? Because the thing is, I'm not attracted to women, sexually, not really. But I'm in love with Sherry, and honestly, it really doesn't matter to me who or what she is."

There was a pause. "What seems complicated to me," I said, "and, forgive my ignorance, but isn't it like being with two different people? I mean, Sherry isn't Sherry all the time, right? Sometimes she's–" I floundered a little. She'd just said the name, damn it. I felt like I was playing a game of Who's On First.

"Sometimes she's Jeff," Megan finished the sentence, and then laughed. "It *is* complicated, for sure. But it's not like it's two different people, no. What I've learned is that it doesn't matter which one she is, because under it all, it's the same person. The person I love."

Rachel said, gently, "You and Sherry have been coming here for a lot of years, though," she said. "You're kind of the poster children for the ideal couple. You've had enough time together to get used to it, right?"

"Yeah, there's that," said Megan. "And for us, the duality of it isn't forever, either, because of the surgery." She caught my eye. "Sherry's going through the process that leads up to gender-reassignment surgery," she said. "Not everybody does, or even wants to. It's one approach. And it's expensive, we've been saving up forever."

"And this…operation…it's okay with her work?" asked Elizabeth, who was still looking at the other women as if she'd started seeing birds flying upside-down. *Alice Through the Looking Glass*. Poor Alice.

"Well," said Megan, "there you've got us. Sherry's lucky, because she's an artist, and that's a way more accepting environment than most others. Actually, you can see her stuff if you want, she displays here in P'town, and in Austin, and she does it as Sherry. And that's not recent, either: she displayed as Sherry, even before she started thinking seriously about gender fluidity; it's just what's always been natural for her. She signed her first painting ever as Sherry. Her artist self has always been female."

"Then she's lucky," said Taisie. "You're both lucky. It's a different world than some people experience. A lot of professions aren't so accommodating."

"Like being a cop," said Elizabeth, so softly it was almost a whisper. There was a painful pause. "Bob's a cop. This would–he never *could*." She looked close to tears, and Megan, who was sitting next to her, slipped an arm around her shoulders and hugged her. Elizabeth took a breath that sounded like it was holding tears. "When you're part of the police force, they make it hard enough for women, for *real* women." She gasped, her hand to her mouth. "Oh, God, I'm sorry!" She was looking at Rachel. "I didn't mean it to come out that way. I meant—"

"I understand what you meant, sweetie," said Rachel smoothly. She didn't look particularly perturbed. "Some people find that they have to change professions. They need to commit to who they are instead of what they do. That's a really hard choice to make. And some people *can't* change what they do, for a whole lot of reasons, and so they spend their lives hidden away, with their real self only coming out at times like this, at places like Fantasia Fair. Which is why we're still needed," she finished, looking at Megan.

"Point taken," Megan said, smiling.

Rachel turned back to Elizabeth. "Who knows how this will play out with you and your significant other?" she said lightly. "Where did you say you're from?"

"Trenton," said Elizabeth. "New Jersey."

Rachel stared at her longer than the remark warranted. She cleared her throat. "A cop in New Jersey," she said finally. "No, I can't imagine that would be easy."

I finally took my first sip of wine. It was really, really hard to wrap my brain around what they were saying. "It seems to me that there's nothing easy about *any* of this," I said. "I mean, I can't imagine falling in love with a man and then afterward…" Never mind understanding; apparently I couldn't even articulate the thought. *Nice going, Riley.*

Rachel snapped out of whatever reverie she'd been in and said, gently, "A lot of women can't do it, for a lot of different reasons. Many of them need a more conventional relationship. Others can't perceive their significant other as fitting into more than one gender role, or understand who they are in such a different scenario." She sighed. "The divorce rate is high."

I was still trying to figure out how I'd feel if Ali announced that his true self was named Allison. We were about the same size; would we start sharing clothes?

Elizabeth said, "I don't know what to feel. I don't know *how* to feel. I don't know how to even walk with him—with her. I don't know who opens the door for the other anymore. I don't know how to—" she gulped "—be in bed together."

Yeah, I thought: that was the crux of it, wasn't it? It wasn't just different genitalia to contend with—not everybody has or even wants the surgery, Rachel had said–it was also a whole way of being, emotionally, sexually, mentally. I looked at Elizabeth and couldn't think of anything to say.

"There are some workshops this week that you can go to," said Taisie. "They're helpful, you'll see. It's tricky as hell to figure out, but take it from me, it's so much better when you're not alone."

"And first thing tomorrow morning there's a coffee hour for non-trans folk who are here for the first time," said Rachel. "In fact, we have that coffee hour every morning throughout the week. Taisie's right, sweetie: you truly aren't alone. There are a number of significant others who've never been to Fantasia Fair before, even if their partners have. And then there are couples in which neither partner has ever been here before, who are doing it for the first time together, like you and–I'm sorry, tell me again your significant other's name?"

"Bob…no. Angela," Elizabeth said faintly.

"So it's for couples like you and Angela, couples who are new to the Fair. Even, for some of them, new to the whole experience. Some older people come here just to try it on, to see if it fits." She sighed. "We don't have

the latitude–we don't give ourselves the latitude, to be honest–that some of the younger
people have. Everyone needs a safe space. I
like to think that Fantasia Fair is totally that
safe space."

"Do the coffee hour," said Taisie to Elizabeth. "I'll come with you, if you want."

Rachel nodded vigorously. "Perfect. It's a
chance to meet each other, and some old-timers, too," she said. "We know that you must
have absolutely tons of questions."

As far as I could tell, Elizabeth was too
terrified to ask *any* questions, much less tons
of them, but what did I know? "*I* have a question," I said. "I'm learning all this, too. You
kind of alluded to this before, but I wonder…When–I mean, if–your significant other
goes through the surgery, what's your cultural
role then?" They all stared at me; okay, so I
was floundering a little here. I tried again. "I
mean, I live here, and I've lived here long
enough to know, for example, that being a
lesbian isn't just about being sexually attracted to other women. There's a culture
there, too." I took a deep breath. "But you
started out as straight…when your significant
other becomes a woman, how do you self-
identify?"

Personally, I think there are a lot of moments—I wouldn't even call them stages—

along the spectrum of the gender one's attracted to, just as I was learning that there are moments along the spectrum of gender, period. And self-identification in one moment can change in another moment. No one's ever completely one thing or the other for their entire life. People grow and change. Well, maybe a Red Sox fan wasn't ever going to dig the Yankees, but in other ways...we become more of who we want to be as we get older. If we're lucky. We're all more alike than we think.

But Megan was nodding. "It's a good question," she said. "And it's not just a cultural question for us, it's a cultural question for them, too. For everyone involved. A lot of cis women have a hard time with trans women being identified as—women."

"That's not fair," said Taisie quickly. "It's when they claim to be exactly the same as cis women that there's been a problem. Like Caitlyn Jenner saying that the hardest part about being a woman is choosing what clothes to wear. And you can't say that was anything but a really stupid remark."

"More than stupid," Megan agreed. "Insulting."

Rachel said, "But you have to put in in context. She'd been an entitled, wealthy, powerful man. She didn't lose the wealth or the entitlement when she transitioned. Most of us don't see her speaking for our experiences, but that doesn't mean that the increased visibility—"

"Wait," I said, putting my wineglass down and holding up a hand. "What's cis?"

Rachel said, "The word is actually cisgender, but it gets shortened. It's a term that refers to someone who gender-identifies as the same gender they had at birth."

"Like you," said Taisie to me.

"Why cisgender?"

Rachel seemed to be the only person who knew. "The prefix means on this side of," she said, "as opposed to trans, which means across from."

"Wow," I said without thinking. "Way to put everyone in a box." Talk about semantics needing to catch up.

"Yes, sweetie," said Rachel gently. "That's exactly what we're saying."

***

There was a disaster in the kitchen.

Martin and Mike were talking about it when I came out of the parlor. "What's going on?"

"It's appalling!" Martin responded. Even his moustache looked affronted. I wondered why I'd never before noticed his resemblance to Hercule Poirot. "I cannot imagine how it's happened."

"It's Adrienne," Mike said to me. Adrienne's the chef at the Race Point Inn's restaurant, and she apparently makes Gordon Ramsey look like a pussycat. Without the expletives, but with her own brand of superior arrogance. Diva didn't even begin to describe her. Or so I'd heard: in my years of working at the inn, I'd never actually met the woman. Which said a lot in itself.

Our paths never had to cross; when I was working on a wedding, I did all the catering work through Martin. He could communicate with Adrienne without contemplating suicide, something I gathered others couldn't manage. For him to be upset about her…"What happened?" I demanded.

Mike shook his head. "This time, it's her favorite knife."

This was bad. There had been a few thefts recently from the inn, notably in the restaurant's supply of cutlery; but a chef's knives are more important to them than their *mothers*. Adrienne came to work with her personal collection rolled up in soft fabric, and left the same way: no one touched her knives. Ever. "It's missing?"

Martin nodded. We were standing near the entrance to the restaurant, and he gestured toward his own station by the door. "They were there–"

"Wait; what? Her knives were out here?"

"Only for a few minutes," he said. "Mike called her to the office. She was carrying them, and another package, and she put it all down here."

"And asked you to keep an eye on it."

He looked like he was about to burst into tears. Even Glenn, the inn's owner, couldn't intimidate Martin like that. He was a maître d', for God's sake, the last bastion of supercilious superiority in the world.

Mike said, "What a hell of a time for this to happen."

Was there ever a good time for this kind of thing to happen? The question was clearly moot and in any case, *I* wasn't going to talk to Adrienne. We were going to have to get that bit straight, right away. But, damn, her *knives*...I couldn't think of what would be an equivalent loss for me; I just knew how losing any of them would–no pun intended–cut deep. "Did they take the whole package?"

Martin shook his head. "No; only one. Her favorite, of course."

"And this happened when?"

"This morning. She wasn't doing lunch today, so it was late, perhaps eleven." The moustache twitched again.

"And you're telling us about this *now*?"

"Now is when she told me about it," he said, affronted.

Mike said, "There's not much that can be done. I called the police. They may send someone out." While losing one of Adrienne's knives might be a catastrophe in our world, I had a feeling I knew how the police would treat the question. I was friends with one of Provincetown's detectives; I could just guess what she would say. "We'll buy her a new one," he added. "But that's not the real problem. The real problem is getting her through dinner tonight."

"Talk to Glenn," I suggested callously. "It's his inn." My phone started buzzing in my pocket. Saved by the bell. "I have to get this," I said, pulling the phone out and checking the caller ID. *Oh, hell*, I thought. *From the frying-pan into the fire.* "Hello," I said, giving Martin and Mike a wiggle of my fingers and turning away.

"So you do sometimes answer your phone. That's a relief to know."

My mother.

"I answer it when I can," I said carefully. I'd been ducking her calls for a week. Damn

Adrienneandherknife.IfIhadn'twantedto get away from *that* conversation, I wouldn't have plunged headlong into this one.

"Well, what did you think of them? Did you like any?"

I slipped into the breakfast room, thankfully empty in the afternoon. "I really didn't pay much attention, Ma," I said. "I'm not in the market for a wedding gown right now." I'd spent much of my adult life dodging my mother's attempts to set me up with someone (anyone, apparently, being better than no one) and now that I had a boyfriend, she wanted to know when we were going to make it legal. This was familiar ground. Next she was going to say something about my profession. Wait for it—

"You'd think that with all the weddings you arrange, you could do something about your own." Bingo.

"You'd think, wouldn't you?" I said. You can't engage with my mother. She has years of dirty verbal fighting under her belt. She could trash-talk any NBA player to his knees. Why my parents are still together is a mystery that baffles me constantly.

The door opened and two trans women came in. One of them caught my eye. "Coffee?"

I pulled the smartphone away from my ear–there's another thing I miss about the old phones, the ability to put your hand over the mouthpiece, who knows where the mouthpiece even *is* on this thing?–to reply. "There's coffee in the bar area."

"Okay, thanks."

She was still talking when I brought the phone back. "...and Amy Lester's daughter got married in September, remember? No one thought *she'd* ever do it, either. Of course, she's younger than you are."

Any minute now she was going to tell me I didn't have many good years left. "Ma," I said, "I'm at work."

"Well, that's part of the problem, isn't it? You're always at work. You're wasting your life at work. I don't know how that man ever gets to see you."

"His name is Ali, Ma." In her desperation to see me wed, my mother had accepted that Ali was probably as good as she was going to get, but she absolutely refused to directly address anything about him, either his Lebanese-American parentage or his religion, which was Islam.

"Well, whatever... The real reason I called–"

Now she was going to talk about Thanksgiving. She had been talking about Thanksgiving since the end of August. Wait for it–

"I wanted to see if there's anything special I should make for your friend at Thanksgiving. I mean, I don't know what these people eat–"

"His name is Ali," I said. "And we haven't really decided about Thanksgiving."

"They *do* celebrate Thanksgiving, don't they?"

I wonder sometimes if I was adopted. This woman and I couldn't possibly share the same DNA. "I have to go, Ma. I'll let you know as soon as we decide. And don't send me any more bridal magazines, okay?"

"You don't want to wait too long," she said darkly. "Liz Perry's daughter was thirty-four when she got married, and they were divorced within a year."

That actually sounded like an argument for my side, but I wasn't engaging. I was breathing. Sometimes I have to remind myself to breathe. Especially when I'm talking to my mother. "Bye, Ma."

It's good that we don't live near each other. I'd have to kill her.

4

By evening, Fantasia Fair was in full swing. The lobby was filled with well-dressed women chatting together, hugging each other, seemingly happy just to socialize. Ditto the restaurant, and I wondered how dinner was getting along, what with the missing knife and Adrienne's volatile nature. Not my problem.

I'm always happy when I run across something at work that's Not My Problem.

I'll admit: I was really liking Fantasia Fair. I was getting to know a group of people I'd understood very little about. I was stepping outside of my usual wedding-related duties and instead just loosely performing hospitality functions that were, truth be told, a lot easier than my usual tasks and worries. And rather than resenting it for taking up my time and attention, Ali seemed to be enjoying it himself; I noticed him at the meet-and-greet deep in conversation with a couple of trans women. "Trans folk," Rachel said when she heard me say that. "The semantics are evolving."

You could say that again.

Megan spotted me and waved me over. "This is Sherry," she said happily, her fingers entwined with those of a tall woman in a business suit. We shook hands. "It's a great inn, dear," said Sherry, her voice noticeably low but not unpleasantly so. "What a fantastic thing, to be able to live here all the time!"

"I'm very fortunate," I said. "I gather you've been coming here for a lot of years."

"Oh, my, yes," she said, smiling at Megan. "We're old-timers, aren't we, honey?"

"We are that," said Megan. "We were going to ask you, Sydney: it just occurred to me after we talked earlier today, but we'd love to have a small ceremony while we're here. We're already married, you know, but we were thinking a renewal of vows sort of thing."

"We'd like to get the language right," said Sherry, nodding. "The wedding ceremony said man and wife."

"That sounds lovely. I'd be happy to arrange something," I said, mentally going through my repertoire of officiants who were available year-round. "Maybe on Wednesday?" That would give me time to get some ducks in a row.

"Perfect!" said Megan. She looked thrilled. My mother would have loved this girl. Maybe.

I looked around for Elizabeth and finally found her, standing alone by one of the windows. "Did you want something to drink?" I asked, feeling that a scintillating opening was called for. Unfortunate that I didn't have one.

She startled. "Oh! Oh, no, thank you. I'm just waiting for Bo—for Angela."

"Where is she?" And why on earth was she leaving this vulnerable and very brave woman alone?

"Upstairs with–I can't remember who. She's borrowing some outfits. We–we didn't have any clothes, and–there was no chance to try anything on, at the stores where we live." I remembered then: her husband was a cop. I could understand their reticence around clothes shopping.

"Well, then, keep me company," I said heartily, signaling one of the waiters with a tray of wine to come over. I'm not a white wine drinker generally, but it was all he had on the tray. "There you go," I said, and gently clinked her glass. "To new clothes!"

"To new clothes," she echoed, bemused. And took a very large swallow of wine. I wondered if they were going to make it, Elizabeth and Angela, or if they were going to add to the high-divorce statistic. Seemed like it could go either way.

"So this is where they're keeping all the interesting people," said a voice at my elbow; Ali. He gave the white wine a quizzical glance but didn't comment on it. "My name's Ali," he said to Elizabeth. "Nice to meet you."

She still looked like things were going too fast for her, and I wondered exactly how sheltered her life was back home. Wherever home was. "Sorry, I should be making introductions! This is Elizabeth," I said. "Elizabeth, my boyfriend, Ali. Elizabeth is from—I'm sorry, I forgot, actually. Where do you live?"

She finished off her glass of wine. "New Jersey," she said. "Trenton."

"Your first time in Provincetown?" Ali asked. He did the social thing really well, I thought. Elizabeth was answering him when

I caught sight of Rachel through the crowd. "Excuse me a moment," I said and took off.

She was bright and busy. "Oh, Sydney, good," she said. "We're going to need an extra room for one of the workshops on Tuesday, it's way oversubscribed, so we're splitting it into two groups. Will that work?"

"We'll make it work," I said. "What a great turnout."

"It's always a fun night, getting to know new people, seeing people you haven't seen for a year or even years," she said. "Oh, here's Lisa! Lisa, this is Sydney, you remember her from the front desk?" The former Bruce, now wearing a bright-yellow dress and bright-red lipstick, nodded. "Good to see you again." Her voice was Marlene-Dietrich husky; again, not unattractive. "I hope you're comfortable here at the inn," I said. "Let us know if there's anything you need."

"Oh, I will." She smiled. "It's already perfect. What a fantastic view of the harbor from my bedroom!"

That was enough conversation for Rachel, it seemed. "More people to meet," she said breezily, her hand on my elbow. "Janice, Sandra, this is Sydney. She does the weddings here. Janice is a psychologist; she's doing that workshop that's turning out so popular this year."

Janice had orange hair. I wondered if it was deliberate or if L'Oréal had failed her. "It's popular every year," she said to me, shaking my hand. "Rachel just chooses to ignore that." What did she do with that hair when she was living out her male persona? Maybe it was a wig. Or maybe she didn't have a male persona. "What's the topic?" I asked instead.

"Intersectionality," she said brightly.

Rachel said, "This is Sydney's first time, Jan, sweetie, give her a break." She turned to me. "It's a term we've borrowed from the civil rights movement—"

"Our movement *is* a civil rights movement," Janice interrupted.

"The African-American civil rights movement, then," said Rachel. "It's relating identity—various identities—to power. Some of our identities are more obvious than others."

I blinked. Maybe I shouldn't have had that glass of wine. "Give me an example?" I suggested.

"Initially it was about the intersection of being black and being female," said Janice. "But it's been extended since then. The point is that we all have vulnerabilities that reflect the intersections of racism, sexism, class oppression, transphobia, able-ism, and more."

It actually sounded pretty interesting, but Rachel was on the prowl. "Gotta go, Jan, she has other people to meet," she said.

"You should come to the workshop," Janice said to me.

"I might," I said.

"It's not all stuff like that," Rachel said. "One of the workshops teaches how to apply makeup."

I might go to that one, too. My idea of getting ready in the morning was comb the hair, brush the teeth, and pass the mascara wand over the eyes. Maybe a little more attention wouldn't go amiss. "And this is Coral. You met her significant other earlier today: Taisie. Coral, this is Sydney Riley from the inn."

Coral looked like a basketball player who'd put on a flowered dress. Awkward but determined. "Don't even look at it, dear," she said, following my eyes. "My favorite dress is missing in action. Loaned it and a couple other things to the newbie."

Rachel was interested. "Angela? That was nice of you. She could use a little encouragement. I think her significant other is having a hard time with it all," she said. "They both could probably use some tips from people who've been around the block a few times."

"Angela's very lovely," said Coral. "So sweet."

"And if she's like most newbies, with *so* much to learn!" said Rachel. "Thank you for reaching out to her, Coral. You're a good egg."

"It's what we do," she said, then caught sight of someone over my shoulder. "Annie! It's been ages!" Quick glance at me. "Excuse me, won't you?"

I stood aside and she swept by. "So many different names," I said. "So many different… I don't know. I feel like I need to have a scorecard to keep them all straight. Oh!" I looked at Rachel. "Was that inappropriate to say? I don't even know when I sound transphobic, to be honest. I don't want to."

"It's a lot to get used to," Rachel said. "Remember that most of us have been thinking about it for a long time, and probably came to the realization of our true gender identity gradually, and then even more gradually chose to claim it. You're trying to get it all in one week. So you might sound phobic sometimes." She shrugged. "It's nothing we haven't heard anywhere else. There's still a lot of hatred out there."

"But I don't hate," I said. "I don't want to add to it."

Mike was suddenly at my elbow. "Have to interrupt," he said. "Sydney, there's a plumbing problem, and Brian's got to be away from the front desk. Can you take over for a while?"

Rachel laughed. "A plumbing problem trumps everything else, for sure!" she said lightly. "Good luck!"

"Sure," I said to Mike. Our working relationship is a little unusual. He's the manager of the inn, but not my boss; I work directly for Glenn, the owner. So instead of telling me what to do, Mike always asks.

There were still people filtering in and I stayed busy for another hour. Ali drifted over, drinking grapefruit juice, and hung out with me. "She's scared," he said.

"Who?"

"That woman back there. Elizabeth."

"Oh." I handed a guest the brochure for our spa. "Enjoy!" I turned back to Ali. "Wouldn't you be scared, with what she's facing?"

"It's not even that," he said. "She thinks that something's going to go terribly wrong."

"Why?"

He shrugged and took a swallow of juice. "She says she has the sixth sense," he said. "Ever since she was a little girl, she's known when something bad was going to happen. She knew the night before her mother died, and before their dog got hit by a car. Premonitions."

"Only bad things?"

"Apparently so."

And what a horrible way to move through life, seeing the darkness coming straight at you. "And probably no one believes her?" I'd always pitied Cassandra, ever since the first time I'd read about her in school. To be required to see the future and know that you will never be believed about it. I propped an elbow on the desk. "And what's she scared of? What does she say's going to happen?"

"Apparently it's not always as clear as the dog getting run over," said Ali. "But she says it's this week, it's soon in fact. She said it was something horrible."

"That's helpful," I said and sighed. "Do you believe in that sort of thing?"

"I've come to believe," said Ali, "in a great many things. My grandmother saw stuff like that, before it happened. It was eerie, the things she knew. Listen: we all only use a fraction of our brains, right? A small fraction, at that. What would we know, or perceive, or understand, if we could use more of it? And maybe there are some people who do. Who can access just that tiniest bit more. Maybe those are the people who spook us the most."

"Maybe." I wasn't sure I wanted to get into the grandmother thing. "Elizabeth really didn't say what it was?"

He shook his head. "Only," he said, "that she saw blood. A lot of blood.

Breathe, Riley; just breathe.

5

By seven nearly everyone had gone, drifting off as couples or in small groups for dinner at favorite restaurants, heading out for clubs and dancing—and you could feel the sheer joy of it sparkling all around them.

Brian having presumably resolved whatever plumbing was causing a problem at the inn, Ali and I headed home. It had been a long time since that sandwich, and I was starving, and my boyfriend is fabulous in the kitchen.

Not that there's much kitchen in which to be fabulous. I'd actually call it more of an alcove than a kitchen. It's not a unique story: what was once a working fishing port with scores of busy wharves was "discovered" (as though it had never been there until the Right People saw it; I'm always bemused when someone says they discovered a restaurant or a book or an idea), first by the artsy bohemian set who turned it into Greenwich Village-by-the-Sea, subsequently by the LGBTQ community, and finally by super-wealthy second-home owners, who loved the quaintness of the place so much that they immediately razed the quaint houses and put up modern condos, making it almost impossible for anyone earning less than a six-figure income to own anything.

So my apartment is just about big enough for me and Ibsen; it probably would have size envy if it ever saw a postage stamp. When Ali's here, it's cramped. But the truth is (and don't *ever* tell my mother I said this), when you're in love, cramped space is just fine.

I poured myself a glass of Côtes du Rhône and him a glass of grapefruit juice and perched on a bar stool to watch him work. "You're out of cilantro," he observed.

"There's no space for cilantro," I said. "Something had to give, and it's cilantro that got the boot."

"Oh, because oregano takes up less space? You have plenty of oregano. You have oregano that will last you through Christmas."

"That's not that far off."

"I didn't say *which* Christmas," he said darkly. "Three jars of it?"

"That's because I forget I have any, and I go shopping and it's sometimes on sale," I said. "And I know what to do with oregano. I have no frigging *clue* what to do with cilantro."

He looked interested. "What do you do with oregano?"

"Put it into spaghetti sauce," I said.

"The kind in the jar?"

I shrugged. "There's another kind?"

"You're lucky you have me," Ali said, and I put my glass on the counter, hopped down from the stool, and stood behind him put my arms around him. "I know I am."

"Huh." He was rinsing lettuce, not to be deterred. "While you're up, can you get the celery?"

"There's no celery."

"There is now. You really think I come unprepared?"

I got him the celery and resumed my perch. And my wine. "What do you do up at the Monument?" I asked.

"Excuse me?"

"Up at the Monument. Even on a day like today, arguably not the warmest day of the year, you go up there and you're away for hours. What do you *do?*"

"Think," he said.

"Okay, I'm thinking."

"Not you, me." He turned and caught my expression. "Ah. A joke."

"Another one bites the dust," I agreed. "So you think. What about?"

He shrugged. "It's a perspective thing," he said, and then put down the bowl he'd been mixing something in. "Okay, so it's about immigration," he said. "Trying to figure out where we went wrong."

"You'd better hope Uncle Sam hasn't bugged my apartment," I said. "That's dangerous talk, these days."

"Any days," Ali said, a little grimly. He turned and leaned against the counter. "I look out there, where the Mayflower was at anchor, and I think about these people and how it all went so wrong."

"It didn't exactly go wrong for them," I said. "The Wampanoag, maybe, but the Pilgrims made out okay."

"I know, I know," he said. "And I know that they didn't come for religious freedom, either, they had plenty of that in Holland. I know they came to make a better living here.

Which you could say for ninety-nine percent of today's immigrants, too."

"You'd better watch out," I said. "Talk like that will get you de-ICEd for sure."

"It just is so…pointless," he said, and turned back to his mixing.

I couldn't argue with him there. Ali used to do things for the government that I thought were pretty pointless, and I had no idea what direction our relationship would have taken if he hadn't transferred from enforcement to investigating human trafficking. It wasn't a pleasant thought. "Well," I said, "at least the view's spectacular."

He made a noise that could have been a laugh. "It is that," he agreed.

Time to change the subject. "Someone got shot last night," I said, and then added, quickly, "Here, I mean. In P'town." Ali's sister is Boston's police commissioner, so someone getting shot wasn't exactly earth-shattering news at *their* dinner table.

"Really?" He spooned whatever he'd been mixing into a casserole dish and put it in the oven. "What happened?"

"Mirela says it was a domestic dispute. Visitors. But the guy's still alive, so either the aim was off or he wasn't really trying. It woke me up last night, I heard it, and I couldn't get back to sleep."

"So," he said, coming over and putting his arms around me. "It sounds like you need an early night."

I smiled. "You read my mind."

***

Monday morning. Even when you wake up next to the love of your life and the weather is amazingly gentle for October and you have interesting things to do, there's never been a Monday morning that anyone's ever welcomed. I'm no exception. There's something inherently discouraging about Mondays, the sense of being a hamster on a treadmill: we finished all this on Friday, and now we have to start it up all over again on Monday? *Really?*

Kind of like clothes. You spend time in the morning picking out clothes and getting dressed, knowing that you'll take them off at night (or, if you're lucky, have someone take them off for you), but that you'll have to start the whole process over again the next morning. Talk about pointless.

I'd staggered into the kitchen and gotten as far as putting the coffee on when the phone rang. Ali moaned and pulled his pillow over his head. I answered, if only to stop the noise. Julie Agassi's name was on the caller ID.

Julie's a cop. Having a cop call you first thing on Monday morning is possibly the one thing that can make a Monday seem–well, more Monday-ish. It was like adding insult to injury. I mentally ran through anything I might have done wrong as I swiped the phone to answer. "Hey, Julie."

"Sydney. I need to talk to you."

"What's wrong?" Her tone had made it clear that she was speaking professionally rather than personally. And when a cop says *I need to talk to you*, you just *know* that whatever follows isn't going to be anything good.

"There's been another suspicious death," she said. Her tone added, "again." Last year, Julie had investigated the death—murder, as it turned out—of my boss, Barry Parker, the inn's former owner and Glenn's life-partner. Granted that Provincetown isn't exactly the murder capital of the world, she still somehow made it sound like I was racking up dead bodies like Jessica Fletcher on *Murder, She Wrote*.

"What happened?" And then, as my mind finally woke up, I added, "It's something to do with the inn?" Because why else would she be calling me? "Oh. God, no. It's not someone here for Fantasia Fair, is it?"

"Maybe you can come down and we can talk about it," she said.

"Where?"

"Johnson Street beach," she said, naming one of the town beaches that nestle in the curve of Provincetown Harbor. "Ten minutes?"

I swallowed. "Okay."

Ali wasn't moving. I hustled into jeans and a cotton sweater, did the quick comb/toothbrush/mascara thing, and was out the door in eight. I took my bicycle–the Johnson Street parking lot is notoriously full, all the way through to November–and headed down.

There was yellow crime scene tape up already, and I had to give my name to a uniformed officer I didn't recognize before he'd let me cross it. A stiff breeze was ruffling the water and spitting up sand and I wished I'd grabbed a jacket on my way out as well. Julie was leaning over something on the beach and straightened when she saw me. "Sydney. Good."

A couple of other people were there with her, one of the doctors from the Outer Cape Health Center, someone else I didn't know, and—to my horror—Rachel Parsons. She caught sight of me at the same time. "Sydney!"

I crossed over to her as quickly as walking in the dry sand would allow. "Rachel." She put her arms around me and hugged me. "I can't believe it. I can't. Even here!"

I disengaged awkwardly and turned to Julie. "What happened? Who is it?"

It was Rachel who answered. "It's Angela," she said, her voice rising into a wail. "Elizabeth's significant other."

"Also known as Robert Gonzalez," said Julie. "And he's one of us. A cop. So this place is going to be swarming with law enforcement before you know it."

"And reporters!" said Rachel. "Reporters who don't understand, who'll sensationalize this, who will make life hell for Elizabeth and—and all of us."

I was starting to grasp the magnitude of the situation. I looked at where Angela—or Bob, or the body, take your pick—was lying face down in the sand. A striking red dress. Red high heels. And the handle of a knife protruding from the middle of the back.

And all I could remember was Ali's voice yesterday, telling me about Elizabeth's premonition. She'd seen blood, she'd said. The same blood I was seeing. Her life-partner's blood. *Breathe, Riley. Breathe, and don't frigging faint.* And there was more.

Unless I was wildly off-base, the knife belonged to a set I'd already seen, wrapped in soft fabric on one of the surfaces of the kitchen at Race Point Inn.

I turned to Julie. "There's something you should know," I said.

6

"Tell me again. You didn't think to report this, because…?"

"What do you think?" I asked, a little defensively. "Things go missing from hotels. It's what happens. We have insurance."

"How much?"

"How much *insurance*?"

She sighed. "How much has gone missing?"

"Who knows?" I took a deep breath and lowered my tone a few notches. "A vase from the front hall. It wasn't Ming Dynasty or anything; we got another from Wildflower and called it a day. There was a timer, some sort of kitchen timer that Adrienne loved and we had to order another one from Switzerland, but that was August." I paused to think. "A clock from one of the bedrooms. And there were some bottles taken from the poolside bar, but we reported those. That was in August, too."

"Anything more recent?"

"You'd have to ask Glenn. Or Mike. Those are just things I know about, because Glenn told everyone to keep our eyes open. This knife–" I swallowed hard. "—it was wrapped up in her knife-case thing and sitting on Martin's station right inside the door. He swears it wasn't there for very long."

"And you're sure that's when it was taken?"

"Of course I'm not sure! I have no idea if it was even there then! I'm not exactly Adrienne's confidante, you know."

Julie shook her head. "But you're sure it's the same knife."

"No, not one hundred percent. I couldn't swear to it." But I could, almost. Adrienne's knives were distinctive. I might not have seen Adrienne herself, but somehow everyone knew her knives. Their handles were, appropriately enough, red.

It seemed to me that Rachel was close to falling apart. "You'll have to talk to Glenn," I told Julie, neatly passing the buck. Glenn owned the inn; Adrienne worked for him. "I have to get her back now," I said.

One of the uniformed male officers snorted and Julie gave him a look that didn't come remotely close to boding well. "You'll be back at Race Point?"

Where else were we going to go? "Yes."

"All right. You can go. I'd appreciate it if you didn't talk to anyone about this."

"But Elizabeth!" Rachel cried. "She'll be crazy with worry."

Julie frowned. "All right." She waved to someone behind me. "I'll come with you."

We found ourselves in a police cruiser for the few blocks down Commercial Street to the inn. Julie was sitting in front, next to the driver, and she half-turned in her seat to talk to us. "When was the last time you saw Angela Gonzalez?" Julie asked.

"I saw her at the meet-and-greet at the inn last night," I said. "And only briefly, long enough to meet. I mean, literally, that was the first time I'd met her." I paused. "She wasn't wearing that dress then, though."

"That's right," said Rachel, nodding. "She changed before going out for dinner. The dress she'd borrowed from Lillian didn't fit very well." Neither of us mentioned how well the red one seemed to have worked.

"Where was she going to dinner?" Julie was taking notes. This wasn't going to be her case much longer: the Staties were no doubt already on their way.

Rachel raised her shoulders. "Who knows? It's not scheduled. Everyone's on their own. And almost everybody has a favorite restaurant, somewhere they go for the first night, like a tradition."

"And what was hers?"

"This is her first time. She's never been to Provincetown before."

If Julie was exasperated, she didn't show it. "Okay," she said as we pulled up to the inn. "Where's everybody right now?"

Rachel looked uncertain, as though she were lost without her clipboard. "Breakfast," I said.

"Right," said Rachel. "Breakfast, and then everyone scatters. The new people have a meeting together, new trans folk and new significant others. Separate meetings, I mean." She seemed scattered herself, not at all like the efficient crisp Rachel I'd come to know during our meetings. "Then there are signups for workshops. There are workshops all day. Here at Race Point, some other venues too. I can get you the master schedule."

"Thanks," Julie said briefly, with a nod. She looked at the cop driving the cruiser.

"You hear all that? Get it from her." She pushed her door open and waited for us to get out. "Ms. Parsons, I want you to gather everyone in the breakfast room and keep them there. I need to see the significant other."

"I'll go," I volunteered. "She's probably in her room still. Where will you be?"

"Manager's office."

Lucky Mike. "Okay," I said.

"Don't talk to her," she said. "Don't say that anything's wrong."

I'm not an expert on what to do in these situations. I've only ever seen one other dead body in my life, and it was last year, at the beginning of summer, when I came down to the pool one Sunday morning and found my boss floating in it. Not a great introduction to the whole murder scene. Even when my *grandmother* died, I didn't see her body.

So now it was two for two. Not that I wanted to make all this about me, but how many people ever see one murder victim, much less two?

We trooped into the inn. Mike was with Glenn at the reception desk, looked over some papers, and they both looked startled as we came in. I gave Julie a despairing look, and stopped off. "One of the guests," I said, as *sotto* as my *voce* could manage. "Her body's down at Johnson Street. Dead." I swallowed. "Murdered."

Glenn kept staring at me as though mesmerized. "Christ," muttered Mike, then saw where Julie was heading. "What…?"

"She has to," I said. "It's one of the Fantasia people."

Glenn found his voice. "This thing has been going on for forty-two years," he said. "It comes to Race Point and someone gets killed."

I nodded. "Yeah."

"Excellent." He looked like he was ready to shoot himself.

I looked toward the breakfast room. "Julie wants me to—"

Glenn nodded and waved me away. "Go on, go on," he said. "Mike, there's going to be media—"

He was already there. "I got it."

"Good."

I hurried to catch up with the others. The breakfast room was full of noise. We do a buffet, a really nice one, and there was a line there, with waiters moving around briskly delivering Bloody Marys and Mimosas and Brunch Punches. There was an amazing smell of coffee. What was wrong with me? I could smell coffee *now*?

And want it even more badly?

Julie had found a bell somewhere. "Can I have your attention, please? Is Elizabeth Gonzalez here?"

Chatter subsided gradually, as conversation after conversation died out around the room. No one said anything.

Rachel was next to me. "She's not here," she whispered.

"I'll see if she's in her room," I muttered, and turned back to the desk. "What room is the Gonzalez'?"

Mike looked at the register. "214."

I headed up the stairs. This was so wrong. These people got to be here for one frigging week out of the whole frigging year and this was what happened to them? My hands were shaking. I remembered how I'd felt when Barry was killed, the sheer bloody self-absorption of someone who thought their life was better than anybody else's. And now here it was again.

I knocked on the door. And again. And again. I should have brought a passkey with me, I thought, as my tentative knock turned into hammering on it. It was clear that if anyone were in there, they weren't answering, and I headed back down the stairs. Julie wouldn't be happy. I couldn't care less. All I could visualize was Elizabeth, scared and vulnerable and seeing visions—that, as it turned out, were eerily prescient.

Just what we needed: Mystic Meg as widow.

Rachel had regained her composure by the time I made it to the breakfast room. She had everyone's attention, was speaking calmly, compassionately. Everyone had to stay there for now, she said. There's been an accident, and the police need to talk to them. Julie and a couple of uniforms were waiting and as soon as Rachel was finished they moved in, Julie with her official voice sounding scarier than most of them had ever heard. Just ten minutes ago the room had been festive; now this.

Rachel came out and saw me and sagged against the wall. "I don't even know what to say," she whispered. "Oh, Sydney…"

I put a hand on her shoulder. Yeah, like that was going to help. "I'm so sorry, Rachel."

"Elizabeth?"

I shook my head. "Not in her room."

"Shit." There were tears in her eyes. "I never thought it would happen here. I've always felt so safe."

"What do you mean?"

"Sydney, this isn't just about Angela. This is bigger than that."

"How?"

"Don't you see?" Her impatience flared. "You wouldn't know. You don't know what we go through. You have no idea."

"I think I understand—"

"You don't understand anything!" she snapped. "Without a safe place to come home to, or a workplace or school where they feel safe, are you surprised that one in four trans people have experienced violence? It happens regularly: violence in bathrooms, violence in other places of public accommodation."

She was nearly breathless. I didn't say anything. "And if a trans person is injured and needs medical care," she said, "they're probably going to suffer *additional* harassment and violence at the hands of emergency first-responders and medical professionals. Or they may even be denied medical care altogether, because of anti-trans bias! And instead of keeping the trans community safe, like they're supposed to, police can be a source of violence. Trans women of color are regularly profiled by police as sex workers, and do you know why? For simply walking down the street! They *must* be hookers, right? You *really* think the police will take this seriously?"

I rounded on her. "Yeah, actually, Rachel, I do." I felt as passionate as she did. "This is

Provincetown. Don't you dare presume that we're like any other community in this country, or even like any other community in the world. We don't do hatred here."

She was beyond thinking about what she was saying. "Oh, because a knife in the back is the P'town way of saying I love you?"

"People get killed everywhere," I said. Sydney Riley, homicide expert. "But whatever it was, they brought it here with them." I paused. "Angela—Bob—was a cop. You really don't think there might be a reason a cop might possibly piss someone off?"

"Not as much as a trans woman would," she said curtly and started to turn away. "See if you can find Elizabeth, okay?"

I think I had my mouth open, but she was already heading into the breakfast dining room. Okay, so tempers were flaring, but I didn't deserve that. Nor, I thought, was it the moment to say so. And Rachel was right: finding Elizabeth was the most important thing anyone could do right now.

Julie was just coming out. "No luck?"

"No."

She looked at me more sharply. "What's wrong?"

I shrugged. "Nothing. Nothing that's important." Or maybe it was; I hadn't really sorted it yet. "What's going on with the fair?"

"They're doing the workshops," she said. "Rachel's in there talking to them now."

"I can't find Elizabeth," I said. "Angela's significant other."

"We'll find her," Julie said. "I don't suppose that you noticed anything last night? Anything that was unusual?"

"Unusual?" I raised my eyebrows. "Julie, I'm new to this. I don't know what *usual* is." I paused. "I only met Angela for a few minutes. But I talked quite a lot with Elizabeth. She was scared."

"Scared?" Her voice was sharp.

"Not what you're thinking," I said. "Not of any person. She was frightened of the whole scene, for one thing. This was the first time they'd come. And I gather that the whole thing was new, that it's only been a few months that Angela's been...well, *Angela*. And then Elizabeth had this conversation with—oh, damn." My hand flew to my mouth.

Her attention sharpened. "What?"

"Ali. Ali's at home. He doesn't know yet..."

"What's Ali got to do with it?"

"It's him she was talking to. Elizabeth, I mean. At the party last night. I'd gone off, and Ali and Elizabeth were talking. She told him she… sees things." I shifted a little uncomfortably. "She said she has the sixth sense, and she saw…well, she saw blood. She said someone was going to get hurt."

Julie was staring at me. "Yes," she said slowly. "I think I need to find this woman."

And I needed, I decided, to find my boyfriend.

7

Ali texted me just as I got to the front desk. "Where are you? Have time this morning for the dunes?" Besides spending time up at the Monument meditating on God only knew what, his favorite pastime was hiking in the dunes. I'd developed amazing muscles since knowing this man.

This situation called for—well, a call; it was way too long for a text. I slid behind the front desk to my little nook and pressed his icon on my smartphone. "What exactly did Elizabeth say to you about whatever it was she had a premonition about?"

He took a second to parse that. "She said she saw blood," he said slowly. "A lot of blood."

"She didn't say whose?"

"Not that precise a premonition, apparently. What's going on, Sydney?"

I took a deep breath. "Angela Gonzalez was killed last night sometime," I said. "There's a knife stuck in her back, and Elizabeth is missing."

"Whew." He paused. "What's Julie thinking?"

"That she wants to find Elizabeth."

"Like maybe she was seeing blood because she was about to kill someone?"

I forget sometimes that Ali used to be in law enforcement; that's where his mind would go. "She'd hardly have told you, would she?" I asked.

"People have done stupider things," he said mildly. "Are you okay?"

"Yeah, I'm fine." Then I caught myself. "No. Not really."

"I didn't think so," said Ali. "Come home."

"But they—"

"If Julie needs you she knows where to find you. Let Glenn and Mike handle this. Come home."

Suddenly that was exactly what I wanted. "I'm on my way."

He had coffee ready and when I got in the door he held me for a really, really long time. I couldn't believe that I was crying. "It's okay," he murmured, his hand behind my head, almost cradling me. "It's okay."

"What's not okay," I said finally, disengaging myself and sitting at the table because I didn't think I could stay standing anymore, "is that Rachel and I had a fight about it. I mean, it's bad enough that someone is dead, but on top of that, she thinks it's a hate crime."

"That's not unreasonable," said Ali. "They're all fantastically brave. I don't know how they endure…and thrive. It must feel to them all like they were born in the wrong time, that a century from now this will all seem perfectly normal to everybody. Instead, they all have to spend their time pushing the limits, trying to show the rest of the world that they're as real and important as everyone else."

"I don't know." I picked at a loose thread in the tablecloth. "Maybe pushing against the limits is the best thing you can do in one lifetime. Moving a culture one step toward something glowing and pure and beautiful

that you won't be around to see, but still be-
lieving that it's been a life worth living."

"Is that what Rachel said?"

"No," I answered. "Rachel wasn't quite
as…positive. But I get it. Her experience has
taught her what people are like. I just got my
back up because it felt like she was insulting
Provincetown."

"Heaven forbid," said Ali, just as my
phone rang. I looked at it and then up at him.
"If I don't take this, she'll just keep calling
back."

"Your mother?"

"Mirela." Same difference, come to think
of it.

He gestured. "Go for it." He stood up.
"I'll make breakfast."

"I'm not hungry."

"You will be."

"As long as there's no cilantro in it!" I
swiped the phone. "Hey, Mirela."

She was clearly miffed that she didn't
know much about the murder, and was determined to find out what she could. "So it is the
wife," she said.

"We don't know that," I said. "She's just
missing. And good morning to you, too."

"So she could be dead also?"

"Don't sound so ghoulish. You're still disappointed that the lawyer who shot himself didn't die."

"All right, sunshine, I will not be so ghoulish. Tell me then. To be honest, are you all right?"

"To be honest," I sighed, "I'm not sure."

"Do you think it is this wife?"

"Do I look like a cop?" I caught Ali's look and lowered my voice. "I don't know. I wouldn't have said she was someone who could hurt a fly, but…"

"Wait. You have met this wife?"

"Well, yeah." Ali slid a small plate in front of me with something puffy and sugary on it. I made a take-it-away gesture. He made an eat-it gesture. He went back to the stove. I went back to the phone. "I spent some time with her yesterday. Well, her and some other women. They were explaining things to me."

"Explaining what things?"

I shrugged. Yep: it still didn't work. Until the time I used video conferencing for everything, I was going to have to give up using gestures to convey meaning. "Explaining about intersectionality. I don't know, Mirela, what do you *think* we were talking about? I asked them what it was like to be married to a man who really in his heart and soul was a woman."

"And this wife, she explained things to you?" Mirela was beautifully unperturbed. If there's anything that shocks this woman, I have yet to hear it.

"No. Well, she clarified the confusion, I guess. They're new at it. Her and Angela, the one who was killed. I'd say Elizabeth didn't really get it all."

Ali put a larger plate in front of me, with some sort of egg and rice concoction on it. I mouthed, "I'm not hungry!" at him and he nodded encouragingly. "Damn it."

"What is it, sunshine?"

"My boyfriend is force-feeding me."

"Ali!" You could have heard her voice in Timbuktu. Wherever that is. "Is Ali there?"

"Either that or he's perfected holographs," I said, and looked at him. "Mirela says hello."

"Tell her I'm in love with her," Ali said, not turning away from the stove.

"He's in love with you," I reported. "Listen, Mirela, as far as I know, they're still looking for Elizabeth. If I hear anything else, you know I'll tell you. But maybe there's not so much of a mystery here. I mean, let's face it, everything I've ever read, anytime anyone gets killed, it's the spouse who's the first one they look at."

"This time may be different," Mirela said. "Because everything about this time is different."

"Different from what?" I demanded. I was eyeing the flaky pastry thing. Okay, so maybe one bite wouldn't be such a bad thing. I could use a sugar rush. I took a bite.

"Are you pretending to not see the 800-pound monkey in the room?" Mirela demanded.

"Gorilla," I said. "It's an 800-pound *gorilla*. Besides, I think the image you want is an elephant. The elephant in the room."

"Zoology and semantics," said Mirela dismissively. "You are avoiding the question."

I took another bite of Ali's concoction and fell in love with him all over again. "Listen," I said, and then swallowed. "I'm not ignoring the politics here, okay? If it's any consolation to you, I've already had my sensitivity lecture for the day, thank you very much. And, gorilla or not, you seem to have me confused with a police officer. I am not investigating this murder."

"Ah, yes," said Mirela. "Like you did not investigate the last one."

"What's she saying?" asked Ali.

"That Julie should deputize me," I said to him. "What is *in* this thing? It's delicious!"

"You are not paying attention to me," complained Mirela.

"Your competition is stiff," I told her. "Something with nuts and butter and sugar and meringue…"

"He is baking for you!" she exclaimed, her voice accusing.

"Sure is," I said. The phone in my hand vibrated. "Wait, I have another call coming in—"

"Do *not* hang up on me!"

"Too late," I said, and switched over. "Julie?"

"Elizabeth is here," she said dryly. "And she says that she won't talk to anyone but you."

***

Ali came with me, this time.

"You seem to attract murder," he remarked as we drove over to the inn.

"Twice in two years," I said. "That's not ridiculous. Your sister probably has two murders a day." His sister is the police commissioner in Boston. I had no idea what the crime rate was in the city, but it seemed like a safe guess.

"The only two in Provincetown," he pointed out.

I glanced across at him. "Maybe it's not me," I said. "Maybe it's the inn. Maybe we're going to get a reputation for being haunted, or something." Knowing our tourists as I did, that would be far from a deal-breaker.

"There's that," Ali acknowledged. "So there's really nothing for me to worry about."

"Is that where this is going?"

He shrugged, lightly. "I have," he acknowledged, "grown accustomed to your face."

"You smooth-talker, you."

There were two police cars in the Race Point forecourt, which pretty much took up most of it. Parking's at a premium in Provincetown. Brian was at the front desk, looking flustered. "Glenn's looking for you," he told me.

"There's a surprise," I said.

"And Adrienne's in the kitchen already," he added, sounding thoroughly alarmed. "I've never seen her here in the *morning*."

Adrienne's presence being, presumably, more frightening than that of the police. Well, he wasn't necessarily wrong there. Brian looked around, leaned in, lowered his voice. "Do you think *she's* the one who killed that guest?"

Adrienne? It was an intriguing and not altogether repelling idea. "Don't know," I said.
"I wouldn't go near her, though, just in case."

He drew back, affronted. "I *never* go near
her!"

"There you go," I said. "Do you know
where Julie Agassi is?"

"Mike's office," he said. "Hey, Sydney, do
you think I can get time and a half pay for all
this? Like people get when they're in danger,
you know?"

"Sure, Brian. This is definitely a combat-
pay situation."

Ali had disappeared, and so I knocked
and went through without waiting to be in-
vited. The telephone call, I figured, had been
invitation enough.

They'd borrowed chairs from somewhere; I'd never seen that many people in the
inn office at one time. Was this some kind of
premature Agatha Christie dénouement?
"You may wonder why I've called you here
this morning…" What were they all *doing*
here? Mike, sitting behind his desk as though
unwilling to give up the authority. Julie, leaning her backside against it. Glenn, in the largest chair and still making it look small. Sitting
close together on the loveseat, Megan and
Taisie. And sitting in one of the armless,
straight-backed chairs from the dining room

and looking considerably the worse for wear, Elizabeth Gonzalez.

Julie looked thoroughly exasperated. "Oh, good, the *wedding planner*," she said. "Just the interrogation expert we need." She had to be pretty near the end of her rope, I thought; Julie doesn't usually do sarcasm. Not professionally, anyway.

I repressed a sudden impulse to say, "You rang?" Instead, I went over to Elizabeth and put a hand on her shoulder. "Are you all right?"

Julie said, crisply, "Mrs. Gonzalez, Sydney Riley is here. You got what you wanted. We're doing you the courtesy of meeting with you here instead of at the police station. Now please tell us where you've been since last night."

She didn't say anything, just reached up a hand and grabbed mine, still on her shoulder. I said to Julie, "Maybe I can talk to Elizabeth alone?"

She shook her head. "Not going to happen."

Glenn cleared his throat; it rumbled loudly enough to make Megan jump. He ignored her and focused on Julie. "Look, Sydney can handle it," he said persuasively. She's the only one Mrs. Gonzalez wants to talk to. Why don't we just get that over with?"

Julie was glowering. She said to me, "she'll have to say it all over again for the state police and the district attorney." So *that* was what was going on: the various law enforcement and prosecutorial entities on Cape Cod generally play well together, but there was a certain amount of pride there, too. Julie wanted to hand it to them all neatly wrapped up.

I nodded vigorously and squeezed Elizabeth's hand. "Of course," I said to Julie. "Elizabeth, come on, let's go talk in the bar." It was the most private place I could think of.

No one said anything and she let me get her out of the chair and lead her from the room. Brian looked like he was about to say something, and then thought better of it. Elizabeth's hand was cold and clammy, like she'd been sweating and then gotten a chill.

The bar was deserted and I pulled a chair out from the one of the tables. "Here, sit here." I noticed a uniformed policeman lingering in the doorway, not watching us but also not exactly not watching us. I sat down. "Are you okay?"

Her dark hair looked stringy and uncombed, and she was clearly wearing eye makeup from last night; some of it had smeared. "I'm...I'm not. I don't know how I am." She sniffled, drew a hand under her nose. Yuck. I managed not to say it. "Elizabeth, what's going on? You know you have to talk to these people."

She nodded.

I tried again. "I'm so sorry about Angela," I said. "I didn't get to know her, but—"

"No!" It was a shout and she was halfway out of her chair and the cop was halfway into the room. I waved him back. "No, no, no!" She'd found some spirit here, somehow. "There's no more fucking Angela, okay? It's Bob. My husband's name was *Bob*. Whatever this was, it's over now. I was married to a man named Bob."

"Okay," I said cautiously. This wasn't the time to talk about Angela's needs; Elizabeth was the one who had to make sense of it in her head. She was the one who had to move forward into the rest of her life. So she wanted to erase Angela. There was something profoundly sad and profoundly disturbing about that, but this wasn't exactly the time to point that out.

And I could also very possibly be sitting with a murderer here. The thought hit me hard; I'd been so busy thinking of comforting her that Julie's obvious interest had passed me by altogether. Elizabeth presented as pitiful and helpless, but maybe that was just an act. Had she decided that the only way out of a situation she considered untenable was to kill Angela? That if she couldn't have Bob, she wouldn't allow Angela to exist?

It made sense in a macabre sort of way. If that were the case, she'd set it up so that she could remember what she wanted... and not deal with the rest. Not allow Angela to come out, ever.

But wasn't that what divorce was for? Just because you don't want someone to exist in your world, you don't have to actually *kill* them to make them go away. What was it that she'd lose back home in—where was it, New Jersey?—that Angela's (or Bob's) death would allow her to keep? And, especially, why was I asking myself so many questions in my head? *Just say it, Riley.* "Okay. Here's the thing. Did you kill him, Elizabeth?"

"No!" She looked genuinely shocked. "No! I loved him!"

I took her hand. So much for not bringing up the elephant in the room. Deep breath. "You loved part of him, Elizabeth," I said gently.

"I know," she said unexpectedly, looking away. "I know." She sounded miserable. Now that I was closer to her, I could smell it, too, the sour odor of leftover alcohol on her breath. Whatever else Elizabeth had been doing last night, she'd for sure been drinking.

"But I think—I think I could have managed it. Eventually." She looked up at me. "I was going to try."

Not exactly a rousing level of support, but I hadn't walked in her shoes. "You have to understand what Detective Agassi is thinking, out there. Usually people get killed by someone close to them."

"Close to them?" Her voice was becoming animated again, and she pulled her hand away from mine. "Close to them? I wasn't close to Bob. He didn't tell me about—this— until just a few months ago. Well, in January. How close is that? He'd been thinking about it and struggling with it and doing online chat rooms about it for years, and never told me. He said he wanted to be sure before he did. Is that close? Is that anywhere near close?"

I moved uncomfortably in my chair. She had a point. "You have a point," I said.

"I wasn't close to him," Elizabeth said. "If you want someone close to him, ask someone here. Or ask *Angela.* All these years he's been seeing this other woman, don't you see that? There's been another woman between us and I didn't even know she existed. I didn't know she was there. But she was in his thoughts and heart for years, Sydney, *years,* and I didn't know it. I didn't have a clue. No; I don't think anyone has to worry about me being—"she sketched out air quotation marks "—*close* to him."

"Okay," I said. "So tell me where you were last night and this morning, and that way she can rule you out and move on to whoever did this."

"Help? You want me to *help*? What do I know? What have I known all along? Nothing! The first time I can help Bob, it's when he's dead, and I can't even help him now." Her brief bout of sarcasm had slipped away and now she was crying, tears running down her cheeks, mascara blurring. She didn't cover her face or wipe her eyes or anything, just sat there and then, suddenly, the tears became a torrent and she was sobbing.

I sat there, ineffectually patting her shoulder and managing not to say anything inane like "there, there," and wondering just how long Julie was going to give me before she decided to take over the interview herself. It felt like it had been a long time. I got up and found some paper napkins behind the bar and brought them back, and she used them once she got to the hiccupping stage.

I waited out a few shuddering breaths, and then said, "Look, Elizabeth, I won't pretend that I understand any of this, or know what you're feeling. That would be massively stupid, and massively dishonest. And it's probably going to be a long time before you'll begin to feel normal again—whatever that is." No reaction. "But first you have to get past today, and the only way to get past today is to tell us where you were last night when Bob was killed."

Her face was now totally blank, as though all thought, all emotion, everything had been drained from it. "When was that?"

I didn't know. "Let's say all evening, all night, this morning," I suggested. That should cover everything.

Another shaky inhale-exhale. "I don't want to say."

Here we went again. I fought down an impulse to yell at her. "Why not?"

No answer. I tried again. "Look, Elizabeth, you have to know that if you don't say anything, that makes you look guilty."

"Maybe I *am* guilty."

Oh, hell. Sweet shimmering scarlet *hell*. I cleared my throat. "What do you mean?"

She glanced at me. "Not what you think," she said. "All right, so I looked around this town for someplace that regular people could go." For "regular," I thought, read "straight, white." Okay, not the first time I'd seen it. I didn't say anything. This wasn't the time for a lecture on diversity. "So I found this bar called the Governor Bradford." *Riley*, I warned myself, *do* not *tell her that the Governor Bradford does drag karaoke. She'll lose it.* "Okay," I said as encouragingly as I could.

"So that's it," she said. "That's all. Bob has Angela, and I wanted something that was mine."

It wasn't hard to connect the dots: it was that simple and that stupid and Julie was going to frigging *love* this. "Do you know—um, what's his name? She'll have to check with him."

She looked at me as though I'd suddenly sprouted wings. "His name?" she asked blankly.

I sighed. "His name, Elizabeth. The guy you met at the Bradford and presumably spent the night with. Julie has to verify that that's where you were."

She wasn't done crying, as it turned out. "I was in bed with someone," she wailed, "when Bob was getting *murdered!*"

While that was undoubtedly true, it wasn't going to help for her to go off the rails again. "It's all right," I said soothingly.

"No, it's not!"

Okay, so it wasn't, and over the next few years she was going to have to come to terms with it, but I wasn't her shrink and I didn't have a clue as to how to deal with this. Plus,

I'd learned what I was there to learn. Except that I couldn't just leave her like this.

She sobbed and sobbed and I thought about what a smart person might say at this juncture, and came up with nothing. I thought about what a detective from a mystery novel might say, and I came up with nothing. I decided that hand-holding nervous brides and grooms was a lot easier than hand-holding someone whose significant other had just been murdered. I decided that I was in the right profession.

By the time I'd had all those thoughts, Elizabeth was getting hold of herself. I got her some more bar napkins. Would she and Angela have managed? Elizabeth was like a lot of people from "out there," who didn't have any direct experience with people who weren't exactly like her: not particularly mean, and phobic out of ignorance rather than hatred. Could they have gotten through that? Who knew? "Elizabeth, I'm going to go talk to Detective Agassi now," I said gently. "She'll want to talk to you some more, and…" Oops. I had no idea what else was in Elizabeth's immediate future. Angela's body would be going to the medical examiner up-Cape in Sandwich. Who knew when it would be released, or when she could go back to New Jersey, all that assuming that her alibi was real. On the whole, I thought it was: this woman had a lot of guilt.

I had more immediate concerns. How was Angela's murder going to affect Fantasia Fair?

Elizabeth, I decided, was on her own.

8

I looked around for Rachel but couldn't
find her; the workshops were, apparently,
proceeding on schedule, though I couldn't
imagine that anyone was talking about anything besides the murder. I couldn't find
Glenn; Mike was consulting with Martin. I
took refuge at my little desk in my little alcove
and felt totally useless. My skillset just didn't
seem to coincide with what was going on.

Ali texted me. "Lunch?"

I hadn't eaten any of his breakfast. The
least I could do was have some lunch with
him. I texted back. "Sure. Where are you?"

"Two minutes away."

What with a slightly delayed reaction to my conversation with Elizabeth, the air of normalcy that he carried with him was comforting. I leaned against the front desk and looked at him critically. He really was terribly handsome. "Behold," I said. "The iceman cometh."

I said it to him at least once every time we were together. One of the reasons I love Ali so much is that he doesn't ever point that out to me. "Come on, the engine's running," he said.

"Enticing."

"Thought you'd think so. Seriously. The parking police will be on it in a minute."

He's right to be scared. Probably in her heart of hearts even Julie's scared of the parking police. They'll ticket in a heartbeat. Especially a big muscle car like Ali's. "Where are we going?"

"Mac's. They have parking. Come *on*."

I settled into the passenger seat next to him. "Hawaiian poke salad," I said happily, naming my current favorite dish at Mac's, the best seafood place in Provincetown.

He glanced at me. "I see that you have your mental priorities straight."

I sighed. "What else can I say? Elizabeth's a mess. She's denying the whole existence of anyone called Angela, all she can say is that her husband Bob's dead, and she picked up some guy at the Bradford last night and spent the night with him, so there's enough guilt there to keep her shrink in sports cars for the next ten years at least."

"One sees why your mind is on the poke salad," he said, nodding.

"And no-one's closer to finding out who killed Angela," I said. There was a short silence. "In a way, you know, I wish it'd been Elizabeth."

That startled him. "Why?"

"Because then it would be just your common or garden variety murder," I said. "You know, no different from when Mrs. Jones knocks off Mr. Jones for his cash and annuities. This way...well, Rachel could have been right, you know? I don't want to even think about it...but it could be a hate crime, after all."

We were pulling into the parking lot. "Cart before the horse," Ali said. "Come on, things will look better once you have some seaweed and raw fish inside you." Ali grew up on Lebanese cuisine and regards my enthusiasm for sushi with a kind of sick fascination. I should have known he had something up his sleeve, taking me to Mac's without being persuaded. We sat at the bar and ordered ginger ales and he cleared his throat.

"And now," I said on cue, "we come to the main event of the afternoon. When you tell me whatever it is that I'm not going to want to hear."

He stirred his ginger ale with his straw. "How do you know you're not going to want to hear it?"

"Deduction. You know my ways, Watson. You know that when you stir it, you make the bubbles disappear, right?"

He stopped stirring. "I'm going back to Boston." He caught my look and shook his head. "It's not because of any of this—well, okay, maybe in a way it is. But if you need me here, I don't have to go."

"Start with why you want to go." The bartender chose that moment to take our order. At Mac's, the Hawaiian poke salad comes with either tuna or salmon; I always order both. You only live once.

Ali handed her the menus. "Thanks," he said, then turned back to me. "There's a case," he said. "And I wasn't next up to take it, but Brenda thought I'd want to." Brenda was the field agent supervisor for the Boston ICE office's human trafficking division. We'd had way too much to drink together one night under the guise of getting to know each other and she showed me her tattoo. There are some things you just can't unsee. "Why did she think you'd want it?" I couldn't imagine too many cases that anyone would *want*. Even when you rescue the victims, even when you shut down the operation, there's no real winning; at best, you're playing whack-a-mole. One a good day.

Last year, when I'd first met Ali, he hadn't yet transferred to human trafficking; he'd been enforcing other customs-related crimes. I think that in some ways he slept better at night, now. And in other ways, maybe not so much. I fully expected him to last another couple of years and then open a garden center or take up carpentry—anything that didn't send screams echoing through his dreams and accentuate the circles that were already under his eyes.

"I told her about this week," Ali said. "You know, about Fantasia Fair."

"Okay." I wasn't seeing anything yet.

He sighed. "Turns out, and I wasn't really aware of the magnitude of the problem, there's a lot of trafficking of transgender women," he said.

"Oh." *That was a little obvious, Riley, wasn't it?* "And a case just came up? Isn't that stretching coincidence by quite a bit?"

"There's always a case coming up," Ali said. "I just haven't been the agent assigned to them. But Brenda saw this and thought about where I was, and—"

"Wait! It's not here, as in here, here? Provincetown?"

"No." He shook his head. "Boston."

Boston. My hometown. Lovely. "Why is it so specific?"

"What do you mean?" We paused while the bartender delivered our meals.

I picked up my chopsticks and played with them for a moment while I thought about it. "I mean, I know that you raid places like massage parlors and so on, places where women are…" I couldn't finish the sentence. "Anyway, are there special places for people who want to prey on transgender women?"

"Everyplace is a place for someone to prey on transgender women," he said. "You really want to talk about this?"

"Not really." I picked up a piece of tuna and ate it, determined to keep my thoughts away from the taste. No; I really didn't want to think about any kind of trafficking. I didn't know how Ali did it. I freak out when I read about trafficking in exotic *pets*, let alone people.

"Okay then." He went back to his clam chowder.

"When do you have to go?"

He touched his napkin to his lips. "Pretty much—"

"Don't tell me: now."

"And *you* know *my* ways, Watson." We smiled at each other.

In a way, I hated seeing Ali go; in another, it was a relief. As it was, I'd been planning to spend a lot of time helping out with Fantasia Fair; Angela's murder was only going to add to that. "There'll be another vacation," I said, picking up rice and seaweed with my chopsticks.

"One that you'll take at the same time as I do," he said encouragingly.

"Absolutely."

"And we'll go away somewhere."

"No question about it."

"Okay, then.

"Okay, then."

We ate in companionable silence.

***

The inn was buzzing when I got back after a protracted good-bye scene with Ali. Rachel was talking to Glenn next to the front desk and she grabbed me as I tried to slip by to my desk. "Gotta see you, Sydney."

Glenn nodded to me. "All right," he said to Rachel. "I'll get the lights rigged for it."

"You're the best," Rachel assured him, then turned to me. "Anyplace we can talk?"

I looked around. There were people everywhere. One thing that an inn doesn't have is *extra* space. Barry had wanted to add extra bedrooms; what we needed were extra public rooms. "Breakfast room?" I suggested.

"Fine." She turned and led the way; Rachel probably knew the inn as well as I did by now. There were a few people in there, chatting, but the loveseat and chair next to it were free, and Rachel headed on over. I had a feeling that I was in for lecture number two. I wasn't really in the mood.

She had other plans. "All right," she said. "Let's start by clearing the air. I snapped at you this morning. That was unbecoming of me. And you didn't deserve it. So I apologize."

I swallowed. "You were right that I don't know enough about the issues," I said. "But, yeah, you were a little forceful in telling me." We exchanged rueful smiles.

Rachel crossed her legs. "I understand that Elizabeth has an alibi," she said carefully.

"That's what I understand, too," I said.

We spent a moment thinking about it. "The Fair is going on," I said tentatively.

She nodded. "The board talked about it," she said. "We decided that it's too important an event to stop. There's talk about it having outlived its use—we're not getting a lot of kids attending, this is really for the older crowd…well, anyway, we all felt it was important for everyone who's here to have the week they planned. The week they need."

The show must go on, I thought, and resisted saying it out loud. "People need it," I said, nodding.

"Yes." She seemed relieved that I understood. She cleared her throat. "The first keynote was this afternoon," she said.

"On intersectionality," I said.

Rachel smiled, something quick and spontaneous and fleeting. "You have a good memory."

"Sometimes," I agreed.

She sighed. "There's so much change in the community," she said. "And behind it all is this common experience, this fear that we all have, of violence. The experiences we've all been through…I bet that, for most people, nothing would feel weirder than having your dad or brother tell you he's now a woman. And for a certain percentage of people, the reaction to that news would be violent."

"That's not so different from us," I said. She looked at me sharply, and I made a palms-up gesture. "What was it you called us?

Cis-women?" She nodded. "I grew up in Boston," I said. "When I was in college, when you went out at night, you were always careful. Listening for steps behind you. Holding your keys so that they'd be between your fingers, in case you needed to punch somebody. Checking men out—discreetly—who were walking toward you. Always thinking that someone assaulting you was a real possible outcome, a viable option. Women grow up walking through life with violence, or potential violence, as an ongoing backdrop to our lives. So familiar that you don't even think about it."

"But no one hated you for what you were," she murmured.

"Really? You really think men rape women because they're so frigging *fond* of them?" A couple of people in the room were looking our way, and I lowered my voice. "It's misogyny either way, Rachel. Men hating women, and men hating people they perceive to be men who don't conform to being a real man."

"That's a little simplistic."

"Maybe. But it's true, too." I took a deep breath. "Anyway. For what it's worth, I'm glad that the Fair's going on."

"Thank you." She glanced at her watch. "Oh, golly. I'd better go talk to Martin." I must have looked blank. "It's the banquet to-night," she reminded me. "They're doing the panel discussion in the restaurant right now, as soon as that's done they're setting up for the banquet."

Adrienne, I thought irrelevantly, must be having fourteen kinds of fits with her favorite knife gone forever; I wondered if Glenn was going to replace it. At least a banquet was easy: one menu for everybody, more or less. She might not even be presiding over the kitchen tonight. "I'll leave you to it," I said to Rachel as I stood up.

"You're coming, aren't you?"

I paused. I hadn't been planning on it, but that was when Ali was going to be in town and we were going to be able to go out to-gether. Or stay in together.

The thought of an evening of Ibsen and the Pad Thai that had been in my fridge well past its expiration date was enough to sway me.

"I'd love to," I said.

9

I got back to my apartment with just enough time to get ready. Ali had taken his car with him to Boston, and mine—a small Honda Civic known affectionately as the Little Green Car—was in my deeded parking place. The walk from the inn wasn't terrible (let's face it, you can walk from one end of Provincetown to the other within an hour, easy), but time was creeping along, as it does.

I jumped in the shower, did the shampoo-and-soap thing in record time, and then just stood there under the hot water, thinking. The truth was that I didn't have a lot I officially needed to do. I had one wedding this week, on Thursday; that was all. The wedding season was winding down and soon, like much of the year-round population of Provincetown, I'd be going on unemployment for the winter. Those who decry unemployment as an entitlement (it isn't, by the way) have never tried to live on it. I usually managed to save enough during the Silly Season to help supplement unemployment and keep me in luxuries like rent, groceries, and heat; but every year it was a challenge. Glenn had promised to pay me for the Fantasia Fair week to do general smooth-the-waters inn-related work, but I didn't have specific functions.

Which left me free, I decided, to see if I couldn't give Julie a hand.

Not that Julie needed one. Julie is brilliant. She was a city detective before coming to P'town, and since our most prevalent crime wave has to do with stolen bicycles, she didn't find herself particularly challenged. So she writes crime novels under a pseudonym—I'm not telling, she swore me to secrecy—and sleeps well at night. Last year she'd started a relationship with a woman we'd both met because of my old boss Barry's death, but that hadn't worked out, and Yasmina had ended up selling her house and moving on.

I'd tried to talk to Julie about it, but she's secretive as hell about her private life, and she does, after all, have her own friends in whom to confide. Many of them overlap with me and the people I hang out with, particularly Mirela—Provincetown is too small a place not to have overlapping circles, layers of relationships and interconnections—but it didn't mean that Julie and I were close enough to talk about broken hearts.

If indeed she had one. I had no idea how things had ended between them.

In any case, Julie was absolutely competent to handle Angela's murder. She wasn't going to be on her own, anyway: in fact, she was going to be officially off the case: the Massachusetts state police investigates on behalf of the DA's office. But wouldn't it be nice if Julie could solve it *before* they did?

Of course, in my heart of hearts, I was substituting my own name for Julie's. Sydney Riley, crime fighter extraordinaire. Not that I'd been so great at helping with the investigation into Barry's death...but maybe practice makes perfect.

Maybe.

Ibsen waited until I was out of the shower and wrapped in a fairly ratty old robe before trying to kill me. He pounced as I turned away from the closet, winding his body around my ankles and sending me to the floor. This happens at least once a week. I looked up at him, the only time when our spatial roles are reversed, and saw the smirk of satisfaction as he began purring. Next pet I have is a goldfish, I promised myself.

I dressed as quickly as I could. I have all these cool skater-style dresses that do look fabulous on me, even if I say so myself; but they all come with a zipper up the back, and when you live alone, a zipper up the back means about five minutes of sweating and swearing through a weird contortionist dance. Ibsen seems to enjoy it; I can sense his amusement. Okay: dress, tights, flat shoes (I don't do heels, for so many reasons I can't even remember them all), a little pinched-waist jacket, a little more attention to makeup and hair than usual, and I was as presentable as I was going to get.

The restaurant looked nice, with tables put together to form larger pods, and fresh flowers on all of them. I'm sometimes hired to do events like this one in the off-season, but this was all Fantasia Fair volunteers, bless them. People were milling about, drinks in hand, chatting, laughing. By now everyone knew that there'd been a murder, but the truth was that no one there had really known

Angela, so there wasn't personal grief around it.

Places weren't assigned, and as soon as I walked in someone called my name. It was Megan, waving from a table not too far from the temporary stage. "Come join us!"

I worked my way over, smiling and nodding to people. I saw a few cops around, none of them in uniform, all of them officers I knew, though I didn't see Julie. That was okay: I could help without actually announcing my intentions to her.

Everyone seemed to have brought out their finery, no matter where they hovered on the spectrum, and I was glad I'd taken the time to do the zipper dance. Megan looked radiant in a blue dress that was clearly designer (though *what* designer, I couldn't say), and her significant other, Sherry, was in a lovely low-cut number that also hadn't come out of any of the places that I shopped. Taisie was there with Coral, and a couple of other people I'd already come to see as familiar; Coral did the introductions. "Sydney Riley, dear, this is Carol Clarkson,"–we shook hands– "and Robyn,"–another handshake– "they've been coming here for *ages* now." That left the lone man across from me. "I'm Sydney Riley," I said to him, as he showed no signs of wanting to join the happy party, which had my junior detective antennae quivering.

He was wearing the usual uniform of khakis and a denim shirt, though he'd dressed it up with something like an Armani jacket thrown on over it. (Note to self: why can I recognize an Armani jacket but don't know the names of the designers who did dresses?) "Henry Tibbits," he said, finally, with a nod. Okay, so that was as far as we were going to get. For now, anyway.

Megan had obviously already started in on the fizzy stuff, and now she reached past Sherry, who was sitting next to me, to pass an opened bottle of champagne. "Go on, have some," she said. "You're not a cop, you can drink on duty, right?" Henry gave her a rather startled look at that, but I acquiesced. No one can accuse me of passing up Veuve Cliquot, no matter who I'm investigating. "We want to talk to you," she said. She was fizzing as much as the champagne.

"Okay," I said cautiously.

Sherry smiled and took Megan's hand. "We just thought it was so fortuitous," she said, "the Fair being here at Race Point Inn this year, and you being involved, and all, so we thought it was a sign for us."

I must have still been looking blank. Megan giggled. "We want to renew our wedding vows," she said.

Yes. Right. *Remember weddings? Your actual job, Riley?* "That sounds lovely," I said. "How long have you been married?"

"Forever," said Taisie, on my other side. "Isn't that right?"

Megan giggled again, but it was Sherry who answered. "Almost twenty years," she pronounced. "We were child-brides, of course."

A wave of laughter around the table, and then the servers were there with the salad course. I thought about doing some sleuthing, but decided to get business out of the way first. I waited until everyone had been served and the rolls and butter had been passed around and people were digging into the greens. "So when would you like to do the renewal of vows?" I asked. "And do you have anyone in mind to do it?"

"Haven't thought that far," said Sherry.

Megan leaned past her again. "You can arrange for a minister, right? Somebody to do the ceremony for us? And we were thinking maybe Wednesday afternoon. Wednesday night's the fashion show, and Sherry's *always* in it." They exchanged smiles. Very cozy. If a romance novelist wrote about a mixed trans/cis couple, Megan and Sherry would be it. "So we thought she could wear the dress she was going to wear for the show to the ceremony."

"Okay," I said slowly. I wasn't following their reasoning, but in nearly five years of arranging weddings, I hadn't yet followed most bridal couples' reasoning, so this was nothing new.

"The rehearsal for the show's from three to four-thirty," Sherry said. "So maybe right after that?"

"Okay," I said. I ate some of my salad and thought about the officiants I liked working with, and who might be available. "I'll see what I can do."

"We know it's last-minute," said Sherry. "But it would mean so much—"

"It's not a problem," I said quickly. The first rule of wedding organizers: never turn down a ceremony. "We'll make it happen." There was a wedding already scheduled for Thursday; Vernon Porter, Provincetown's inimitable Lady Di, was performing that one. I liked to spread opportunities around, so I was thinking Dianne Kopser, who was one of the chaplains at the Unitarian Universalist Meetinghouse. Plenty of time to get that arranged.

Someone was going to have to bring up what Mirela called the 800-pound monkey in the room. Taisie waited until the plates were cleared. "Did Elizabeth go home, does anybody know?" she asked.

Coral, sitting between Taisie and Henry, shook her head. "That poor dear woman," she said. "She must be devastated."

"I don't know," said Taisie doubtfully. "She wasn't very happy to start with."

"She was new," Megan said. "We've all been there. You can't blame her for that."

Across the table, Henry cleared his throat. "Are you talking about the woman who got killed?" he asked. I liked him immediately for saying woman so naturally.

"Her significant other, dear," said Coral to him. "It was their first time here." There was a pause while everyone waited for Henry to say it was his first time, too, as the two couples clearly didn't know him—and they were Fair devotees, they would have. He didn't oblige. "Is she a suspect? The wife?"

"I don't think," I said primly, "that any of us knows what the police are thinking. But I know one thing—Elizabeth does have an alibi."

That got me a lot of interest. "Really?" asked Megan, and, "that's good to know, dear," said Coral almost at the same time, and in the midst of it all, the main course was delivered, which in my case was salmon. With pomegranate seeds in a glaze on top. Odd combination, I thought; probably not Adrienne's doing. Unless the use of her favorite knife as a murder weapon had put her off her game. That would be understandable, after all. I waited until everyone was served, and then said, "I don't know how official it is, but from what I've heard it's pretty clear that she's out of the running as a suspect."

"I can't imagine she'd ever have been one," said Taisie, cutting her chicken with small sharp jabbing movements, as though to get the task over with quickly. She took a bite, swallowed, and added, "Seriously. She wasn't the type."

Henry looked at her with mild interest. "What's the type?"

"I don't know." She twirled her fork in the air. "Someone ruthless. Someone determined. Someone who didn't mind getting their hands dirty. Someone who's focused and maybe even desperate. Elizabeth's just too…too perfect. And mousy, you know? She probably can't step on an ant without agonizing over it."

Someone said something else, but I didn't hear it. I was staring at Taisie, her words reverberating. *Someone who didn't mind getting their hands dirty.* Of course: there was going to be blood. A whole lot of blood. Elizabeth had said so herself. Multiple stab wounds, and who knew what internal organs got hit, but there would have been blood, lots and lots of blood. Somewhere–maybe in Agatha Christie–that the first stab is "free," but that after that, there would be blood spatter. It wasn't just the killer's hands that were going to get dirty; whoever it was, they were going to be, literally, a bloody mess.

On one hand, it made sense, logically anyway, that the killer was connected somehow with the Race Point Inn; after all, they'd managed to steal an incredibly protected and important knife from well inside the premises. (And why? Wouldn't any knife have done the trick? What was special about a chef's knives?) On the other hand, I didn't care who was on the front desk that night, if someone had passed them dripping with blood, even the most distracted of night clerks was going to notice.

So they didn't go past the front desk.

It wasn't impossible, of course. The inn is fairly rambling; Barry bought it back when property in Provincetown was still affordable and it has a lot of space: several bars, two dining rooms and a restaurant, a pool—now closed for the season—a spa, and a whole lot of rooms, many of which could be accessed via keycard from a number of different entrances.

But the connection with the inn was just too strong to ignore. "Excuse me," I said to the table, earning several startled glances. Taisie had been speaking; I'd interrupted her. "I just have to make a call," I said, pulling my smartphone from my bag and standing up. "I'll be right back."

Out in the lobby I pressed Julie's icon. "Agassi," she answered immediately. "This had better be good, Sydney."

"Why, did I interrupt a romantic dinner?"

A snort. "Not while I'm attached to a homicide investigation," she said. "What is it?"

"I was just thinking that whoever did this is connected to the inn," I said. "And that there had to be a lot of blood involved. I mean, they could throw the knife into the harbor, but it's a little cold to throw *themselves* in." The annual Swim for Life, which starts out at Long Point and comes in to the beach at the Boatslip, is at the beginning of September, and even then most of the participants are wearing wetsuits because of the cold. In October? Not a chance. "So I'm thinking that they might have cleaned up in their room, and so if all the towels didn't get down to the laundry yet…"

"Thanks, detective," said Julie. "We did actually think of checking that, though I appreciate your advice. Is that all?"

I felt deflated. "I guess you didn't find anything?"

"Nothing I can share with you right now," she said crisply, which could of course mean anything. "Is that all?"

"Yeah. I mean, no. Where's Elizabeth?"

Julie sighed. "Sydney, what are you doing?"

"Trying to help. You're not making that very easy, I have to say." I took another tack. "You know anything about some guy called Henry Tibbits?"

Another sigh. "Why?"

"Because he's sitting at my table at the Fantasia Fair banquet, and he doesn't exactly blend into the landscape. I thought he might be one of yours. Undercover, and all."

"Not a very good undercover if he sticks out as much as you think," she said. "Sydney, I know you mean well. But—"

"Do *not* tell me to let the grownups handle this."

"Where's Ali?"

"Aha," I said. "I say grownup and you think Ali. Why, is he supposed to have some sort of maturity that I lack?"

"I was just thinking," said Julie, "that you might share your thoughts with a trained investigator first, see what he thinks of them. That's all."

"So I was right," I said. "You're saying let the grownups handle this."

"And you are proving my point. I'm hanging up now, Sydney. Have a good banquet."

I clicked off the phone and glowered for a moment. I was seriously annoyed, and I knew that it was mostly because Julie was right. Of course the laundry would have been an obvious place to start, even when–maybe especially when–Elizabeth was the prime suspect. So if I was going to be of any use at all, I was going to have to up my game.

I was slowly realizing that this wasn't just an intellectual exercise for me, or a way of filling time when the wedding season had slowed to a trickle. Angela's death had meaning. She was just at the point of coming to grips with who she was, of starting to actually *celebrate* who she was, to feel comfortable in her skin, to be natural and real and relaxed– maybe for the first time in her life–and someone had taken that away from her.

I remembered another conversation I'd had with Julie, back when Barry had been killed. I'd wondered, then, how anyone could live with murder on their conscience. Julie had been bemused at my innocence. "The person who got killed was inconveniencing their precious little life. The person they killed was standing between them and financial ease, or a different spouse, or whatever it was that they wanted. They were so self-absorbed that everything was about them, and that justified doing whatever they needed to be happy."

So whose plans had Angela disrupted? Who was she getting in the way of?

Of course, Julie hadn't been talking about hate crimes, which were a category all to themselves.

I went back to the banquet. Champagne had given way to wine, which was now being supplanted by coffee as dessert was served. Tiramisu. Okay, maybe I could stop investigating for a *few* minutes.

It was not to be. Coral was continuing a conversation that seemed to have been flowing since I'd left the table. "And you know she'd have to be a newbie, dear, to wear heels on the beach," she said.

"Seriously!" Sherry exclaimed in agreement, laughing. "It's a good way to break an ankle!"

I slipped back into my seat and took a bite of tiramisu. Waste not, want not. "What are you talking about?"

"Angela on the beach," Taisie told me. "We don't even know why she was there."

"A lot of people walk there in the evenings," I pointed out. "People walking their dogs, people wanting some quiet time…" People wanting some not-so-quiet time, too, though *that* part of the beach was infamously on the other side of town from us. The town beaches—as distinguished from the ocean-side beaches, administered by the Cape Cod National Seashore—were havens of calm that stretched all around the curving Province-town harbor shoreline. Over on our end, to the east of the piers, it's calm most of the time; the fast ferry from Boston and the whale boats round Long Point and head straight for MacMillan Pier. Over here, it's as quiet as can be.

The ideal place, perhaps, for a murder.

"What the lighting like?" That was the enigmatic Henry. "I didn't see any lampposts."

"There aren't any," I said, still wondering who the hell he was. "There's light from the Johnson Street parking lot, and probably some from the buildings—there are condos along there, some shops, the Harbor Lounge on one side, and Pepe's on the Wharf on the other, but…"

"But what?"

I shrugged. "Pepe's is two floors of outdoor dining in the summer," I said. "But even with the industrial heaters, it's chilly enough that there probably weren't a lot of people out there." And this, too, was probably ground that Julie had already covered.

"Still," Henry said thoughtfully, "it doesn't seem ideal. There'd be no way of knowing who else might come along at just the wrong time."

"Or the right time, depending on your point of view," said Taisie.

"They must have thought it was the best chance they'd get," he said. "With all the group activities going on here, it would be very difficult to get somebody alone. They'd have to take advantage of any opportunity they got."

I put down my fork. "All right," I said to Henry. "Who the hell are you?"

10

"I know that we've all been enjoying the great hospitality of the Race Point Inn," Rachel Parsons was saying into the microphone up on the stage. "And I'd like to bring out the inn's owner, Glenn Rogers, for a round of applause by way of saying thank you."

Everyone in the room started clapping. Glenn shambled up on the stage, big, bearded, self-conscious. Rachel pulled him over to the mike and air-kissed him and he looked like he was going to pass out from embarrassment. "Thank you," he muttered. Really. That was all. Next year, I found myself thinking, we'd have to get Mike to do the

honors. He was at least slightly more accustomed to public speaking. Or maybe I could
spend the winter making him practice, a sort
of DIY Toastmasters.

Glenn escaped and Rachel resumed her
spiel. "Fantasia Fair is now in its *forty-second
year*," she said, and applause burst out again
sporadically around the room. "Yes... thank
you, thank you, I know, I know! Can you believe it? So welcome, one and all, to Fantasia
Fair, a week-long celebration of gender diversity and the longest-running annual confer-
ence in the transgender world!" More
applause and a few hoots. This part, I realized, was like every banquet speech at every
club in the world. I could snooze through it.
Or, alternately, eat the tiramisu.

Rachel was nodding. "I won't keep you
from your dessert and after-dinner activities,"
she was saying. "But I want to celebrate our
history together and maybe inspire some of
the young people among us."

She was going to have to look long and
hard to find a lot of them, I thought, glancing
around the room. There were a few people
under thirty. Not a lot.

"In the early 1970s, the transgender community as we know it today did not exist,"
Rachel said. There were a lot of nods around

the tables. "This was a time when the Stone-wall Riots were still recent memories and when a man found dressed as a woman was subject to ridicule, social oppression, and, in many places, even arrest–or, worse, death. Many people falsely assumed that being gender-variant and being homosexual were the same thing, and that both were mental illnesses. Most transgender individuals were isolated, afraid, and alone. A few reached out to one another and corresponded through letters and newsletters. Some secretly met on occasion to form small social groups, such as Freedom of Personality Expression and the Mademoiselle Society.

"In 1975, Fantasia Fair was conceived in response to what was then articulated as a need for cross dressers and transsexuals to learn about themselves in an open, socially tolerant environment," Rachel said. "Provincetown was chosen to host the event because of its reputation for tolerance, and because it had become a gay and lesbian Mecca. With some help from a couple of female impersonators who lived in town, some doctors practicing on Cape Cod, a few cosmetic consultants, and about 40 participants, Fantasia Fair went from an idea to reality."

Hoots, applause, stamping on the floor. They were loving this, I thought. I'd been wrong, before: this wasn't just another banquet speech at just another civic organization's annual meeting. This was lifeblood. This was not just a history, this was their history. As Rachel went on through the forty-odd years of Fair lore, hands moved to hold other hands under the table, handkerchiefs came out, an occasional sob or sigh could be heard. This was their family's genealogy, being recited just for them. And Angela, who would have been hearing it for the first time, was missing out on feeling part of something bigger than herself.

It made me angry all over again.

Rachel was done with history and was moving into the current state of affairs. "Things have changed for the better, there's no question about that," she said. "But we have such a long way to go!" Nods from all over, and beside me, Sherry said, quietly, "Oh, Lord, yes." Rachel looked around the room. "Here's how trans women usually show up in pop culture," she said. "A straight male character hits on some woman at a bar, only to find, surprise, surprise, that the woman is actually transgender. And from that point on, it's played like it's the straight male's worst nightmare. And the man's hilarious" (she air-quoted with her fingers around the word *hilarious*) "negative reaction is always the point of the story: it's all about *his* panic, *his* anger, *his* disgust. The trans woman is just a prop. And in every case, we're meant to identify with the guy. He was attracted to her, and since she turned out to have a penis, that attraction was, of course, an intentional dupe on the part of the transgender woman."

Still sounded to me like we had a lot in common. Women who say no to men's advances often get the same reaction.

"That has to change. We all agree: popular culture needs to see us as it does anyone else. The gay community has started to make inroads there; now it's our turn. And if they're not going to do it for us, then we'll do it for ourselves!"

More rousing applause.

"People say that we reached a transgender tipping point a couple of years ago," said Rachel. "Janet Mock and Laverne Cox made Americans sit up and take notice." She paused. "And then, there came Caitlyn Jenner." Mixed reactions this time, some cheering, a few groans. Rachel picked up on it right away. "I know, I know," she said, making pacifying gestures at the room. "But she had the juice to make Americans realize that there was a revolution going on. That was a good thing. At the same time, you can't understate her extreme privilege as a wealthy white woman who started out as that most privileged of people, a wealthy white man. You have to contrast that with the lives of most trans women, who continue to face extreme discrimination that pushes them into poverty, ill health, abuse, and even death."

She took a deep breath and looked around the room. "And that brings us to what has happened to one of our own," she said. "Our sister Angela Gonzalez was killed–murdered–last night, on the first night of an event meant to celebrate who she was and who she was becoming. I know that many of you are angry and sickened by this." Another pause. "I am also angry and sickened by this," she continued. But I have two things to say to you tonight. One is that we do not know the facts about what happened, and when you don't have the facts, it's easy to make assumptions, and sometimes even to act on those assumptions. So I urge you all to stay solid. Stay calm. Stay unified. We will know eventually why Angela died, and who killed her, but until then, speculation and anger will not serve our community well."

She let the silence reverberate for a moment. "The other thing I want to say is this. Several of you have approached me about discontinuing this year's Fair. Out of respect for Angela, you're saying." She took a deep breath. "Angela Gonzalez got her respect when she checked into this inn. Angela finally got to a space in her life where she could leave the masquerade behind, where she could come here among us and be herself. I know that many of you feel the same way. We have a wedding scheduled for this week. We have a renewal of vows scheduled for this week. We have learning and networking and celebrations scheduled for this week. There is no better way, to my mind, to honor Angela and celebrate her life than to dedicate this year's Fantasia Fair to her!" Applause, people on their feet: Rachel knew how to work a crowd.

I was clapping, too. It felt like one of those moments, those moments where you believe that there's a chance that everything will actually be all right, after all. That no matter what they do in Washington, no matter how bad it gets everywhere else, Provincetown was a magical place where people could take those steps into something good and pure and real. Where even disagreements could generate light, not heat.

I found myself saying it, like a mantra. *Light, not heat.*

Angela had found the light. And it was up to the rest of us, I thought, looking around the dining room at the faces flushed with wine and food and sentiment, to not translate it into heat.

But where did you start with something that big?

***

I started with Mirela.

After the banquet I grabbed the heavier jacket I keep in the office for emergencies and wandered down Commercial Street. The Johnson Street parking lot still had yellow crime-scene tape around it, so I didn't go down to the beach. Instead I walked out onto MacMillan Wharf, where the fast ferries and whale boats and fishing charters docked on one side, and what was left of Provincetown's working commercial fishing fleet docked on the other. Boats with names like Donna Marie and Terra Nova and Jersey Princess and Antonio Jorge, boats that were there year-round when the other non-commercial boats had all fled south, following the warmth down to the tropics.

For tonight, there was still activity on both sides: the Dolphin Fleet didn't head south until the end of October, and even the two sailing schooners were still doing sunset cruises. For people who bundled up well. Everyone was in by now, though: it was dark, and all I could hear was the wind slapping ropes against masts, water lapping at the sides of the boats. The big pier lights were on and created circular pools of brightness beneath them.

I went down to the end of the pier and sat on a bench and looked out at the lights of the town winking all around the curve of the harbor. And then I called Mirela.

"My poor sunshine, are you all right?"

"Of course I'm all right," I said. "Why wouldn't I be all right?"

I could feel the shrug. "Well, with Ali back in Boston…"

"How do you *know* these things?" I exclaimed crossly. "Seriously, Mirela. Where are you now?"

"In my studio. I am working," she said piously.

"And what, you're a telepath?"

"Ali called me, sunshine," she said. "He is worried about you. He thinks you will become involved with the murder investigation."

"Well, he's right," I said.

"He told me to watch out for you."

I raised my eyebrows. "And this is how you watch out for me?"

"I am doing it in spirit, sunshine. What was it you wanted, since you called?"

"Someone stole the head chef's favorite knife from the dining room and used it to stab someone else on the Johnson Street beach," I said. "Someone who particularly didn't deserve it."

"No one deserves it, sunshine."

"But Angela less than others, even." I wondered how she'd felt on the way to Provincetown, arriving here, the excitement of finally doing it. Her last day on the job, putting on the uniform in the police locker room, everything so clearly masculine and stifling, with the secret of Fantasia Fair simmering in her heart.

At least she'd felt that. At least she'd been in a bright scarlet dress when she died.

"Perhaps." Mirela is from a country where violence is, if not accepted, then at least expected. I tease her and Ali about their close friendship, but I know also one of the reasons for it: Bulgaria is a hub for human trafficking into the European Union. There are reasons she doesn't live there anymore.

I sighed and watched a boat motoring slowly in, its lights bright on the water. "It's so complicated."

"Why? Why is it complicated? What you said is simple."

"Don't forget that 800-pound monkey." I was quite enjoying her malapropism.

"Nothing is simple in the context. There's so much controversy and conflict over the whole trans issue. You can't just separate it out, you know. There is so much ignorance and fear, and they add up to violence. Well, that or stupid bathroom laws."

"Then," said Mirela, "you must look beyond the context."

"I don't think—"

"Oh, sunshine, shut up. My paint is drying. I do not have time for this silly argument. If you are going to insist on thinking about this, then think correctly. No one outside of this group knew this person would be here, yes?"

"Not even people *in* the group," I agreed, "until she got here."

"So. It was probably not a random guy on Commercial Street who saw her and lost his mind over issues of gender and killed her, yes?"

"Okay," I said cautiously. "When you put it like that…"

"I do put it like that. So you can ignore the context. A hate crime, this is about a group of people. Listen. This knife, it was difficult to obtain. This person was alone perhaps for only a short time. Or had gone walking on this beach with someone else.

This was personal, sunshine. You are looking for politics where there is only human folly."

I don't know anyone else who can actually say "human folly" and carry it off. But she was also right. Her argument had enough holes in it to create a fishing net, but what if she were right? I hadn't even thought about the reasons people kill other people. I remembered, again, the conversation I'd had with Julie. Money, or love. Self-centered reasons, reasons that were petty and greedy and mean. *Think small, Riley. Very small.*

"Sydney? You are still there?"

"Yes," I said. "I'm here. I'm just thinking."

"Then think alone. I have work."

"Okay," I said and sighed. "Thanks, Mirela."

"Be careful, sunshine. I do not want to tell Ali that I did not protect you."

"Oh, I wouldn't worry about that," I said. "No one wants me dead."

Well, I was *partially* right, anyway.

11

So here's what I think. The truly important things happen in the margins of our lives, in the moments when we least expect them to, when we're really not paying attention. Maybe that's a defense mechanism, so that later we can say, oh, I didn't really mean that, or oh, that didn't really happen. Because they're so important that to look at them would change our lives completely.

I wasn't paying attention the next morning. Maybe I hadn't been paying attention the whole time.

***

Every single morning I swear I'm going to change the wake-up tones on my smartphone, and every single night I do nothing about it. Talk about self-sabotage.

It's an annoying little sound. Maybe any wake-up tones would be irritating–who really ever *wants* to get up, after all?–but that Tuesday morning I grabbed the phone and hurled it across the room. It's to be noted that I have a well-padded case for my smartphone especially for moments such as this.

I opened my eyes. Ibsen was gazing placidly into my face. He was sitting on the pillow next to mine. Nothing like waking up to your beloved's furry face first thing.

So far, nothing about this morning was particularly appealing.

I staggered around a bit, making the bed, percolating coffee, pulling on jeans and my WOMR sweatshirt, brushing my teeth, feeding the cat. The bare minimum.

With her unerring sense of timing, my mother chose that moment to call. I let it go to voicemail. She called back; voicemail again. On the third call, I finally picked up. "What *is* it?"

"See!" she said triumphantly. "I *knew* you were there!"

I sighed. "What is it, Ma?"

"So now I need a reason to call my daughter?"

"You *always*," I said, "have a reason for calling your daughter."

She sighed. No one sighs quite like my mother. You can feel *layers* of guilt in those sighs. "You haven't told me about Thanksgiving yet," she said.

"Ma, it's October," I said. Seriously: Thanksgiving in Antarctica would be preferable to Thanksgiving with my mother. And my father, for that matter, though his sole contribution to the festivities would be the ritual carving of the turkey.

I don't even like turkey.

"So some people like to make plans in advance. So they don't inconvenience other people," she said. "I have to order the turkey from Drumlin Farms, you know."

"And this is my problem—how, exactly?" I demanded. "I haven't even talked to Ali yet about the holidays. We're both working a lot."

"I was going to make your Aunt Celia's sausage stuffing, but your father said those people don't eat pork."

Oh, my God. I'm going to kill her. Over the phone. "It doesn't matter, Ma. We're not talking about Thanksgiving yet."

"So I thought I could do the cornbread stuffing instead. It's not as moist, but it's tasty and we've had it before, it makes nice leftovers."

There was a click on the line. Yes, there is a God, and he loves me. "I have to go, Ma, I have another call."

"And this is polite? Hanging up on me because some other call is more important?"

You got it. "Bye, Ma." I clicked over without looking at Caller ID. "Hi, this is Sydney."

"Hi. Hi, Sydney. Um—this is Elizabeth. Elizabeth Gonzalez."

Wasn't she back in Trenton? "Hey, Elizabeth." I made my voice as gentle as I knew how. "Are you home—um, I mean, where are you?"

"I'm at the Race Point Inn." She sounded puzzled. "Where should I be?"

"I'm sorry. I'd assumed that you'd gone home." *Well, duh, she wouldn't have exactly gone to the banquet last night.*

There was a noise of some sort that she made in her throat and that I couldn't interpret. "They haven't finished with—they haven't released Bob's body yet. I want to wait for that. I want to take him home." She paused. "They'll do the funeral there. Even if the officer didn't get killed in the line, they'll still do a beautiful funeral."

"I see." And what questions were going to be raised at his precinct? She was going home to a nightmare. "What can I do for you, Elizabeth?"

"I wanted to say something. I mean, I thought...oh, I'm sorry. This is coming out all wrong." She took a breath. "I'm not comfortable with Detective Agassi."

You and a bunch of felons, I thought. Julie could be intimidating. "Do you have something she needs to know about?"

"Well, not a thing, exactly...I just..." She took a deep breath. "Yes, actually, she should know it. But I don't know how to talk to her."

I sighed. "Do you want me to come see you?" I asked.

There was no mistaking the tone this time: gratitude. "Oh, yes, please! Would you?"

I looked at the laundry I needed to do and my cat who was shredding the sofa because I wasn't around much and nodded. *Right. She can't see you, Riley.* "Give me half an hour," I said.

"Oh, thank you! Thank you, Sydney. I'm in room 214."

I couldn't really blame her for not wanting to meet in any of the inn's public spaces, I thought. I probably wouldn't want to hang out with anyone, myself, in her place. "See you soon," I said, and disconnected. I caught Ibsen's eye. "What? First my mother, and then you?"

He meowed his discontent.

***

Brian was at the front desk when I arrived. "Oh, good," he said when he saw me. "Can you take over?"

I looked at him suspiciously. "Why?"

"Because I need a break, and my boyfriend's coming over to take me for pizza."

"Who's supposed to be here?"

He looked disgusted. "Emily."

"Oh." Emily was a recent hire, and the only good thing to say about her was that we hadn't hired her during the season, because if we had, all hell would have broken loose. The Race Point is open year-round, but we staff up for the summer; Emily had started in September. And probably should have ended then, as well. "Isn't there anyone else? I actually have something I need to be doing."

Brian did a graceful stretch; he'd been with the Boston Ballet until first an injury sidelined him and then Provincetown—and, presumably, the boyfriend—seduced him. "Not that I've seen," he responded. "Glenn and Mike are around somewhere, and Martin, too. I suppose you could get someone from the spa, but this is it for me: I'm out of here for an hour." He ducked under the counter and appeared again on my side. "Good luck, sweetie," he said.

I stared after him. This day was just getting better and better. I smiled automatically for a group of Fair guests drifting by and chatting together while I punched Mike's icon on my phone. "Brian just went on break," I said.

There was a lot of noise in the background. "Why are you telling me this?"

"Because he just left and Emily's not here and I have someplace I need to be."

"That's right," he said. He shouted it, really. "You need to be at the front desk!"

"Mike!" I glanced at the guests sitting in an alcove across the way, turned my back, and lowered my voice. "You can't do this to me."

"Sorry to ruin your day," he said. "I have bigger problems right now."

"Where are you?"

"Basement. Shit, watch that, will you?" It was a howl. "We've got some pipe damage down here, Sydney, I can't worry about people going on break right now. The cellar's gonna flood in another few minutes."

"Hell." I knew when I was outmatched. "All right." I disconnected and slipped behind reception and used the house phone to call Elizabeth's room. I wasn't going to be able to give her the privacy she wanted, after all.

I let it ring twelve times before giving up. All right, so she'd changed her mind. It wasn't my problem. *My* problem was that, apparently, today everyone else's problems were becoming mine. My mother. Elizabeth. Brian. Mike. I ticked them off in my head while I smiled pleasantly and gave directions to the Monument (Rachel hadn't been kidding about that one), information on Tea Dance at the Boatslip, and a Band-Aid to someone with a paper cut.

You can't say my life isn't glamorous.

I grabbed my loose-leaf wedding book and called the chaplain from the UU, Dianne, about Wednesday's renewal of vows ceremony. I thought about what I was going to say to Emily if she showed up, and decided that for both our sakes it would be best if she didn't. Rachel drifted by, consulting the clipboard as usual, giving me a vague smile. "Have you seen Elizabeth?" I asked her.

She stopped, thought about it. "Yesterday," she said. "Come to think of it, she was looking for you. Poor lamb. She seems totally lost."

"Can't imagine any other response," I said, shrugging. "It's rotten that she feels she has to stay on. This must be unbearably painful for her. If the police will let her go, we should encourage her."

"But the support network here—"

"–isn't hers," I said firmly. "She's got her own support system back home. Family, friends. She only just met us all on Sunday, and under circumstances she wasn't exactly delighted about."

"Well, there's that," said Rachel.

"I'm going up to see her after Brian comes back to cover reception. I'll talk to her about it, see if there's anything we can do to help," I said.

"Good, good." She seemed preoccupied. "Is everything all right?" I asked, then mentally kicked myself. It's such a stupid question. They ask it on TV all the time. If everything were all right, there would have been no need for the question, would there?

Rachel didn't seem to mind. "One of the workshop facilitators left," she said.

"Left–as in resigned?"

"It's not exactly a job, you don't have to give two weeks' notice," she said sharply, then relented. "I'm sorry. I'm a little on edge." She sighed. "It's sure going to be a memorable Fantasia Fair, isn't it? And for all the wrong reasons."

"People turn to each other in crisis," I said reassuringly. "Some good will come out of it." Wow. I was really on top of the truisms this morning.

Rachel left and I tried Elizabeth's room again. Maybe she'd gone for a walk. Maybe she was just sitting on the bed, staring at the telephone as it rang. I'd done that, in my time.

I wondered how things were going in the basement.

Brian came back, bearing a peace offering: a slice of pizza from Spiritus. You can forgive someone a lot when they bring you pizza from Spiritus; but it was going to have to wait. I left it on my desk and headed upstairs and knocked the door. "Elizabeth! It's me, Sydney!" I tried again. "Listen, I'm sorry I'm late!"

Nothing.

Well, she could have gone out. She could have *checked* out, for all I knew.

I went back downstairs. Brian was on the telephone with a guest, assuring them that extra towels were on their way. "Passcard?" I asked as he hung up, and he gave me the keycard that opens all the doors at the inn. "Can you take some towels up to 132?"

"Get someone from the spa," I said. I was suddenly, sharply, wanting to make sure that Elizabeth was all right. She wouldn't have hurt herself, right? I was imagining pill vials and a bottle of Scotch by the time I got back up to her room. Surely not. And she knew I was coming, and so could save her, and then I hadn't come on time… The keycard took three tries to work. *Breathe, Riley, don't panic, just breathe.*

And then the door was open and I was falling into the room and Elizabeth was on the bed, only there was no Scotch and no pills, only the marks around her neck and her eyes staring vacantly up at the ceiling.

12

She was dead soon after she'd called me.

That was what Julie said, anyway, and I wanted to believe her. I couldn't stand the thought that I was standing uselessly down at reception and could have, maybe, saved her.

"You could have maybe ended up like she did, if you'd gone up sooner," Julie said. "Get a hold of yourself, Sydney. This isn't about you."

No. This was about Elizabeth. "She wanted me to tell you something," I said miserably.

"Yeah? What was it?"

"I don't know." I caught her look. "No, really, Julie, I don't. She didn't feel comfortable talking to you."

"She's a cop's wife and she didn't feel comfortable talking to a cop?"

I shrugged. "I don't know what was going on with her. I just know she felt comfortable talking to me, and she wanted to tell me something to pass along to you."

"Hmm." She looked around the room. They'd moved Elizabeth's body, and the air felt still, vacant, empty. Whatever had been here was gone. "Seems like someone didn't want her saying whatever it was she had to say."

"So she did die because of me!"

"Oh, give it a rest," Julie said. She grabbed my shoulders and made me face her. "Look at me, Sydney. It didn't matter who she was going to talk to. And maybe what she was going to say didn't matter. *We don't know anything right now.* Okay? And you're no use to anybody if you're going to disappear into a morass of self-pity."

I drew a shaky breath and counted to three. Recovered somewhat. "A morass? Did you really just say a morass?"

"It was the best I could do at the time. Are we good? 'Cause I really have some work to do here."

I nodded. "We're good."

"Okay." She released my shoulders and I fought an impulse to rub them. She has strong hands. Which led me of course to thinking of the hands that had been around Elizabeth's neck...I turned away and stumbled out the door. I was not going to be sick. I was not going to be sick. I was not going to be sick.

Yeah, right. I made it to the restroom at the end of the corridor. Just barely.

I cleaned myself up and washed my face and stared at myself in the mirror for a long time. I wish I could say I was thinking deep thoughts. I wasn't. It was all going round and round and round in my head and none of it was making sense. What was it with this couple? They come to Provincetown for the first time ever, meet up with people for the first time ever, and both get *killed*?

I turned around and propped my bottom on the edge of the sink. Angela had been a cop in New Jersey. I didn't know much about New Jersey, but thanks to various movies and TV shows, I associated it with crime, especially organized crime, in one way or another. Sorry, New Jersey: I'm sure that you have some nice communities, too. So. A cop in New Jersey. Couldn't Angela's past somehow have caught up with her? Someone following her here and killing her to keep suspicion off—the Mob?

Not that the Mob ever had any problems owning up to its body count. Besides, there was one very big problem with that scenario: unless someone knew P'town well, a hired killer would stand out here like a...well, like a hired killer at Fantasia Fair. Everyone here at the inn had preregistered; and I couldn't imagine someone not connected with us managing to both steal a knife and get into a room. The first time I'd met Ali, he'd been wearing a suit, and I remembered thinking how odd it looked; we're a laid-back sort of place, sartorially speaking. Men just don't wear suits here.

Of course, a hired killer didn't have to wear a suit; that was TV lore speaking again. But I was still pretty convinced that this wasn't just Angela's past catching up with her...and with Elizabeth. It had to be something to do with being here, with the Fair.

Before, I'd thought that being part of the investigation would be a way to pass my time. To help Julie. To help the Race Point Inn. Like a hobby, like the hundreds of protagonists of cozy mystery series who solve crimes in their spare time for fun.

Elizabeth had twice chosen me, specifically, to talk to. Had chosen *me*. Had felt that

I could give her something that no one else could. And the first time, I'd come through. Julie was right: this wasn't about me; but that didn't mean that it wasn't personal for me. Perhaps not personal in the way that Barry's death had been; but personal nonetheless.

I took a deep breath, tossed my paper towel into the rubbish, and pushed open the door to the corridor. *Bring it on, Miss Marple.*

***

Ali sounded distracted. "Hang on a second so I can find a quiet place to talk," he said, and a few moments later, "okay, now I can hear you."

I pressed my smartphone to my ear, which is singularly silly since the sound doesn't come out of the flat part. And someone says it gives you cancer of the brain, holding it next to you like that. And why was I thinking such stupidly irrelevant thoughts? "So isn't it true that killers find one way to kill people and stick with it?" I asked. That's what every mystery novel I'd ever read seemed to indicate. "The modus operandi?"

There was a pause. "I have no idea how to answer that," Ali said. "Is there a context here I should know about?"

I took a deep breath. "Someone killed Elizabeth Gonzalez," I said.

"I see."

"I see?" I was sitting outside in the patio/garden area where we usually staged our weddings. Going for the familiar. The good thing was, no one else was out here. "Is that *all*? She's dead, and you *see*?"

"Sydney," Ali said, forced patience in his voice, "I'm sorry. I have a lot going on here. What do you need?"

We'd agreed, from the beginning, that work came before anything else. In the year and a half that we'd been together, we'd respected each other's professional life. For me, it was the urgency of couples planning the best day of their lives. For Ali, it was...something else, something darker, something I didn't want to think about. "Oh, God," I said, something cold seizing me around the middle. "You have a container full of dead bodies, don't you?"

That's me: zero to the-sky-is-falling in three seconds flat.

"No," he said gently. "No container. But we do have some problems. Tell me what it is you need from me."

"Angela was killed with a knife," I said. "And Elizabeth was strangled. Doesn't that argue for two different killers? Don't they

150

pick one way of doing things, and stick with it?"

There was another pause. "You do know, don't you, that I don't work homicide?"

"But–"

"But," he said, "I think you're thinking about serial killers, Sydney. People who kill for the pleasure of it. That's something that's completely different from most killings, and I'd venture to think completely different from this one." He sighed. "Here's the thing: despite what some of the cop shows you watch would have you believe, there really aren't that many serial killers in the world."

"The ones we know about," I said darkly. Someone told me once that any criminal who gets caught is the stupid one. The smart ones are the ones who aren't caught. The really smart ones are the ones who commit crimes that never even get identified as crimes.

"The ones we know about," he agreed. "I don't think you're looking at someone who kills for pleasure. I think you'll find at the end of the day that there was a reason for it. Maybe not a good reason, but a reason."

"But that doesn't explain why once they used a knife and then they–strangled–"

"Sydney," he said calmly. "I need you to take a deep breath. Now." He waited, and I breathed in and obediently out a couple of times. "Now listen to me. It's extremely unlikely that you have two killers running around Provincetown. What is probably happening is that the person who killed Angela planned that murder enough in advance to secure the knife. Yeah? And then found out at the last minute that he had to kill Elizabeth, too, and there wasn't time to plan anything, he had to just work out something on the fly. That's all."

"Okay."

"Are you all right? Because I really have to—"

"Go," I finished for him. "Yeah, I'm okay. Sorry. I shouldn't call you at work."

"Call me tonight, okay? I'll have more time to talk then."

I nodded. He still couldn't see me nod. "Okay," I said.

"I love you."

"I love you, too," I said, and disconnected the call. It made sense, what he was saying. The same person, backed into a corner and using whatever was to hand. In this case, literally: his hands.

I just wanted to cry. To bury my face in my pillow and have Ibsen snuggled next to me and cry and cry and cry. I forgot sometimes how protected we are in P'town, how insulated from people who did awful things.

And I was such a girl. All I wanted to do was cry.

Miss Marple would be *horrified*.

13

Downstairs I ran into Coral. Almost literally. I was looking for Rachel and came around a corner and there was Coral.

"What's going on?" She was dressed in daytime wear: jeans, a lacy top, lighter on the makeup. Still wearing heels. She grabbed my arm and pulled me out of the way of anyone passing by. Which no one was. "Why are the police here again?"

I sighed. Aside from the sheer awfulness of everything going on, it was starting to occur to me that this was, among other things, a public relations disaster for the inn. House of horrors. Inn of death.

Breathe, Riley.

"I don't know if I'm supposed to talk about it," I said, "but I don't really care. It's Elizabeth Gonzalez. She's been–"

Hand over her mouth. "Oh, my God!"

I nodded. "In her room," I said. She seriously looked like she was about to pass out, and I put a hand to her elbow. She grabbed it and it felt like she'd only broken one or two bones. "I need a drink. Can we get a drink?"

"Of course." I managed to get my hand back and steered her toward the Small Bar, as we call it, though come to think of it, it actually isn't all that small, it's just that...*stop it, Riley.*

Gus was behind the bar. He'd gotten fired last year (and had even been momentarily suspected of Barry's murder), but was back...Glenn said he was turning over a new leaf, trying to attract different sorts of people to the inn, and Gus was part of it. Gus was flamboyantly bisexual, if that makes any sense, flirting with men and women alike with great gusto. The guests adored him. Personally, I thought the jury was still out on his use to the inn, but what do I know? "Coral, my darling!" Gus exclaimed.

"Hello, dear. I've had a shock," she said, gliding gracefully onto the stool. This girl had had practice; that was for sure. Not her first bellying-up.

"The usual, then?" She nodded and he looked at me. He knew *her* usual, and not mine? I'd have to forgive him, due mostly to the fact that I don't actually have a usual. "Stella," I said. A mixed drink seemed excessive, and wine too celebratory.

Coral was dabbing at her eyes with a real handkerchief. "I just can't believe it, dear," she said to me. "It's like some horrible nightmare."

"Hotel of the damned," I said, nodding. I'd gotten to the point where if I couldn't find some humor in all this, I was going to take those pills myself.

"Something like that."

Gus presented her with something frothy and pink in a martini glass, then offhandedly opened my bottle and offered it to me. Tentatively. "Glass," I said firmly, and he poured it and set it in front of me. "Cheers," I said, and took a sip.

"I suppose," Coral said, "that we're all so lucky, in a way, dear, just to be alive."

It was a thought that hadn't occurred to me. "We are," I said. "Something to remember every day."

"Yes, but now especially." She took a hefty swallow of her concoction. "It just makes you think about death, doesn't it? And the luck factor, dear. It's all luck."

Well, that and not pissing somebody off enough that they wanted to kill you, I thought.

Coral took another swallow that nearly drained the glass. "I mean," she said, "that I'm the luckiest one here."

Oh, God, was she going to get maudlin about her marriage to Taisie? That was the fastest-working alcohol I'd ever seen. "Why is that?" I asked and took another sip of beer.

"Well, you know, here's the thing," she said, finishing off her drink. "Gus, dear, I think I'll have another."

I held up my hand. "In a minute, Gus." There was something going on here, and I wasn't quite getting it, but there was something... "What are you talking about, Coral?"

"Well, it all makes you think about death, dear," she said again, her voice trailing off. Then she seemed to get hold of herself and shivered. And laughed. "I'm being ridiculous, aren't I, dear? But, see, it was my dress that Angela was wearing. Remember she came here without anything, and she was too self-conscious to go shopping, even here, so a bunch of us got together and we each loaned her our very favorite outfit. For good luck, or something, I don't know. And it was my dress she was wearing when she got killed. My dress, my shoes, that's my favorite red. And I just keep thinking, wouldn't it be scary if the killer mistook Angela for me, dear? Like it was supposed to be me who got killed? But now… well, I hate to say it, of course, dear, but I'm kind of reassured by Elizabeth, because it was haunting me, that thought that somehow I was responsible for Angela dying. And now I know I wasn't, and it's such a relief."

"Not to mention," I said before I could think it through, "being reassured that no one actually *does* want you dead."

She stared at me. "That, too, I suppose, dear," she said. "Can I have that drink, now, please?"

Gus whisked her glass away and did his magic and gave her another candy-colored concoction. I sipped my Stella and thought about it. I could remember it now, of course, the conversation on Sunday about Angela not having any suitable attire. And how unutterably sweet it had been for everyone to give up their favorite outfit for her week among them.

Sweet, and possibly deadly?

I looked at Coral as she sipped at her glass; she seemed calmer, now that she'd told someone that thought that must indeed have been haunting her. Here I'd been whining that Elizabeth's death could have had something to do with my being stuck at the front desk (*oh, and Riley? What if you'd arrived sooner? You think they wouldn't have killed you, too?*); Sherry had a very real concern that Angela might have died accidentally in her place. "That's a lot you've been holding onto," I said.

She shrugged. "I couldn't tell anyone, dear," she said. "Taisie wouldn't have understood. She was pissed off enough about the dress. We paid a lot for it, dear, and it's not like I'd ever wear it again, even if the police did let us have it back, which they won't."

I was curious. "Did you ask?"

"Taisie wanted to. But I didn't."

Yikes. Dead person's clothing. Then again, I do a lot of shopping at thrift stores; I'm probably at any given time wearing something that had once belonged to someone now deceased. I remembered, vaguely, when people were protesting the fur trade, I was in Boston and saw a sign stuck to the plate glass window of the furriers on Newbury Street: "The previous owners of these coats were murdered while wearing them." Not quite the same. I couldn't blame Coral; I wouldn't put the red dress on again.

Then again, red really isn't my color.

***

I decided, after that, it was time to actually do my job. A novel concept, I know, in view of my activities over the past couple of days. I called Dianne and arranged a meeting with her and Sherry and Megan right after lunch, and then I took off on my own. I needed time away. Away from people, away from questions, away from even my own thoughts.

In other words, Quality Cat Time.

Ibsen was, for once, obliging. I lay on my sofa and he curled up on my stomach and started purring, and I closed my eyes and imagined myself in my happy place. Well, it's not actually a place: my happy place, my favorite fantasy is simply imagining–remembering?–being on a swing. Back and forth, that delicious rush of air as you go forward, kicking back with your legs, the feeling of the rope in your hands, the sweet smell of newly

I could go on like that for hours.

***

Mirela called around four. "We have dinner plans," she informed me.

"We?"

"You and me."

"I don't know," I said, feeling a little vague and wooly. "I don't really have time. I'm trying to figure out what happened at the inn. I need to be there. I need to help Julie."

"Julie," said Mirela decisively, "has the Provincetown police department, the Massachusetts state police, and probably the district attorney's office working with her. People who know what they are doing, sunshine. She doesn't need you."

"Thanks a lot," I said. "*You're* remarkably well-informed."

"I just know what is what, sunshine. Come to Caroline's house."

I took another tack. "I was just in the middle of a lovely fantasy."

"Oh, good, you can share it with all of us."

"Mirela—"

"Caroline's house," she said firmly. "By six o'clock."

Caroline Sousa has lived in Provincetown forever. She's from one of the old Portuguese fishing families; her generation has given up the sea, but she paints the boats now, in oils that sell well at one of the most successful galleries in town, all angles and dark colors, harbingers of danger and disaster. She owns a big house in the west end that she inherited from generations of fishermen who each added onto the house before the Historical Commission had anything to say about listed buildings, and for her friends, it's always open house there. She has a wide generous porch with a glider and tables and ferns, and I can't count the number of summer evenings I've spent on that porch, looking out as sunset touched the harbor and drinking pitchers of margaritas or sangria.

And come to think of it, there was no better way I could imagine to spend my time right now.

I didn't go back to the inn. I went to the gym, and sweated through weights and cardio and spent fifteen minutes in the steam room, feeling my muscles relax, one by one.

You can do a lot of thinking while you're working out in the gym. I did none at all. I put in my ear buds and listened to Ani Difranco and Tori Amos and Anna Nalick. I sweated. I reached no helpful conclusions. I picked up a decent bottle of Côtes du Rhône at the package store, got on my bicycle–there wasn't a dream of parking in the west end, even in October–and headed over to Caroline's.

Sunset. Visual artists come from all over the world to capture this moment. There's something about the light in Provincetown, they tell me: something unique and extraordinary that's drawn artists here for decades, from Hawthorne to Hensche, from Webster to Hofmann. And even though I've lived here for years, sunsets—especially autumnal ones—never get old. In fact, in the wintertime, it's a social occasion: if you go to Herring Cove, where the sun sets into the water because of the curve of the Cape, you'll see a line of cars in the parking lot, everyone sitting in them (it's far too cold to stand outside) and waiting for the sky to do its nightly show. "Will you be at Sunset tonight? See you then!" is a common enough remark in the dark days of November through March.

Sunset from Caroline's porch is lovely. Here the sun doesn't set into the water, but instead its fantastic light illuminates everything—harbor, boats, birds—in warm shades of gold, picking out minute details that you'd never see at noontime. There were already a few people there when I arrived, sitting in Adirondack chairs and on the porch glider, balancing paper plates filled with potluck on their knees. I made my way through to the kitchen without falling into too many conversations, and eventually was out sitting on the porch with a plate of assorted and totally incompatible foods and a glass of red wine. And that fantastic light.

Almost as good as being on a swing.

14

Okay, so here's a tip: never go to a social event in a small town when you are at the center of anything interesting. You won't get a minute's peace.

At least I wasn't getting any. I had garlic shrimp in my mouth and was feeling pretty good about everything when it started. "So, Sydney, what's the latest?"

I swallowed my shrimp and frowned. Adele Anderson was looking at me rather intently over the rim of her glass, and this was significant because Adele Anderson did some freelance writing for the Cape Cod Times. "I don't know," I said cautiously. "I'm not the police."

"Oh, come on!" It was Caroline, next to me. "You're right in the middle of it all. You have to tell us *something!*"

"What I want to know," said Carrie Bridges, wearing a hoodie, sitting cross-legged on the floor, and drinking out of a beer can, "is why anyone would go walking on the beach in high heels."

That struck a chord: someone else had been talking about that. I couldn't remember who. Or whom, as Mirela would insist.

"Like you'd know anything about high heels!" Carrie's partner Lisa was saying, and everyone laughed. "Still," Carrie said, "it's a question, isn't it? Maybe he was walking somewhere else, and the body got moved."

"I think the preferred pronoun is she," I said mildly and bit into another shrimp. I knew where the conversation was going now, with this group of friends that included lesbian, bi, and straight women. Hell, I was helping to steer it there. Starting them talking about gender politics would take the heat off me to Tell All. I do have my ways.

I wasn't wrong.

"She!" snorted Carrie. "Right. Wearing clothes that are all about what men think women should wear."

"High heels that keep you from running," said Sarah softly. We all knew she'd been sexually assaulted a few years back, before she moved here.

"There you go. A rapist's dream," said Carrie.

"It's not just about the clothes, though," said Caroline. "You have to be fair."

"Fair? Straight men wearing a straight man's idea of female beauty and pretending they can own it? You don't find that repressive? As a feminist, that doesn't bother you?"

"As a feminist, *drag* bothers me," said Caroline. "I'm not so sure about this."

"Like there's a difference!"

Oh, hell. I was going to have to engage, after all. I opened my mouth to respond and before I could, Mirela said, "But there is a very big difference. Look at how you are dressed. You are dressed like a man. It is not a parody, you are not wearing an Edwardian costume, you are dressing like a regular man. Because that is what is comfortable for you. You wear jeans and boots and sweatshirts. Because it is how you feel best."

"Yeah, Carrie, when's the last time you wore a dress?" It was Lisa again. I wondered if there wasn't some undercurrent going on between the two of them.

"That's completely different. You can't tell me anyone feels more comfortable wearing a dress and high heels."

"And you," said Mirela, "cannot tell *me* that they do not."

"But to get back to Sydney's point," said Caroline, "dressing like a woman doesn't mean that you *are* one. You can't just assume the pronoun."

"Why not?" I asked. I was finished with the shrimp anyway. I took a hefty swallow of Côtes du Rhône–I had a feeling I was going to need it–and drew my knees up, which I could do since I, too, was arguably dressed as a man in my black corduroys and desert boots. I cleared my throat. "Aren't you the same women who want to talk about herstory instead of history? You're choosing to frame your own experience, change language that you experience as oppressive. Why can't someone else?"

"Because they're taking something that belongs to us!"

I blinked. "You own the language?"

"Someone has to," said Carrie, sounding exasperated. "And owning the language is owning everything. It's how Republicans thrive, because they get in there first and frame the issues, own the language. Democrats don't *get* that." She sounded frustrated.

"Listen, Sydney, I get it that we need to have some solidarity here. But when Caitlyn Jenner–" there was a collective groan from everybody "–says something ridiculous, like the hardest thing about being a woman is choosing which clothes to wear, well, that's just plain insulting. It is; you *know* it is."

She had a point. "But that's one person. One idiot."

"Who speaks for a community."

"Who speaks from a place of entitlement," I snapped. "Listen, Bruce Jenner was an entitled white man with money and fame. So what did you expect, he'd be any *less* entitled once he transitioned? And for every Caitlyn Jenner, there's probably a thousand people, a lot of them kids, who don't have money or fame or the security Caitlyn has. They get thrown out of their homes. They lose jobs or housing, or can't *get* jobs or housing. They're trafficked." I spared a thought for Ali, doing God only knew what to try and stop the trafficking. Like I said: whack-a-mole. "They're killed. They're vulnerable to everything bad that can happen to a human being, and I can guarantee you that not a single one of them has ever thought that the hardest thing about being a woman is picking out what to wear next!"

There was a short silence, after which someone behind me started clapping slowly. "Nice speech," she said, and I recognized the voice: Elaine Summers, who works at the library and writes feminist science fiction. "So, because so many bad things have happened to this community, we should say that they can't do anything wrong? That's bullshit." She moved closer in to the circle, elbowing Mirela to move over on the porch glider. "Listen," said Elaine, leaning in. "People who haven't lived their whole lives as women shouldn't be the ones who get to define us."

"Hear, hear," said Carrie.

"They're not defining us, they're defining themselves," I said.

Elaine shook her head. "Look, I recognize men's rights to reject cultural ideas of maleness," she said. "And I'm cool with where they want to go with that, if they're gay, if they're trans, if they're bi, it's all cool. If they're straight and just like girly things, that's cool, too. I think that little boys should be able to dress up in their mothers' clothes and play with Barbies."

"And you wrote a whole novel about a planet where that happens, too!" said someone, and we all laughed.

"But what's not right is this: they can't find their dignity by trampling on mine," said

Elaine. "That's the bottom line, for me, at least. Your truth is my truth, all of you, because you've all moved through the world as girls and as women with everything that that entails. They haven't. They haven't had business meetings where the guys at the table address their remarks to your breasts." She was ticking things off on her fingers. "They haven't forgotten to take a pill and freaked out because they might be pregnant. They haven't learned that the guy sitting in the cubicle next to them doing exactly the same thing they are makes twenty thousand more a year than they do. They never worried about the embarrassment of their period coming unexpectedly and inconveniently. And straight men never–" she looked pointedly at Sarah "–needed to worry about a date turning ugly, or violent, or deadly."

"They had just as many problems, though," said Lisa. There was a gleam in her eye: she was winding people up, and again I wondered what had been happening between her and Carrie. "Some of them worse."

"I'm not denying that," snapped Elaine. "I'm not going to compare notes and say, hey, which of us is more oppressed by the patriarchy? I'm just saying that it's not the same, and they can't step in and define me any more than I have the right to define what a male experience is."

"But isn't that what female-to-male trans people are doing?" asked Sarah. "We don't talk much about them."

A bubble of conversation, laughter. "Yeah, 'cause who would *want* to be a man?"

"Rhetorical question?"

"You said it!"

"Seriously," Mirela said, "Are there no male trans people at the Fair, Sydney?"

"I think one or two," I said cautiously. "I haven't seen them around much, though."

"So there you go," said Elaine. "Again, my point. Women are socialized differently than men. So trans women think they can own the space, while trans men are still busy trying to convince everyone they have the right to exist."

"It seems to me," I started to say, when Caroline Lewis, who'd so far been quiet, interrupted, "That's bullshit, and you know it. They're getting male privilege. They're going over to the other side."

"The other side?" echoed Sarah. "When did it get to be us versus them?"

"Since Adam and Eve, honey."

"It seems to me," I said again, and Sarah snapped, "We're not helping the discourse

here. You don't solve anything by being dis-
missive."

"Oh, like the way men are with women?"

"Can I say something?" I yelled. There
was a startled silence. I took a deep breath.
"It seems to me that everyone's taking the
whole trans verbiage to an extreme. It's not
either/or. At least not with the people I've
met. They're good people, they're kind-
hearted people, and they're just doing what
everybody else is doing, trying to figure things
out. So most of us here are comfortable in
our skins. Whether we're gay or straight or bi,
how we perceive being women, who we are
as women, we've made some peace with it. So
how in the hell can we talk about something
that we haven't experienced, and then try to
fit it into neat little boxes?"

I took another steadying breath. "Saying
trans may work, but talk about language, talk
about framing an issue, it sounds like a journey between two extremes. And, hell, if
there's anyone who should understand the
limitations of binary thinking, it's women,
right? What's useful about talking about a
spectrum that has two extremes?" (Even
though, I reminded myself, I'd used the word
spectrum easily enough myself when talking
to Ali about it.) "Everyone wants to put other
people in boxes with labels, but labels hurt

everybody, and they don't work. They just don't work. Just like for some people, sexuality can be fluid, gender can be, too. For some people, being trans–that is, being in transition–is the journey, but for some people it's the destination. They don't need to be clear to other people. Sometimes life is just a little messy. And, by the way, the best way to learn about someone isn't to sit on a porch talking about them, but to listen to what they want to tell you and try to treat them the way they want to be treated, without putting your version of reality on top of theirs."

There was a long silence, and then Mirela said, "Okay. Good. So, sunshine, can we talk about the murders now?"

***

I was halfway home when my phone rang. I pulled my bicycle over to the side of the street, thinking it would be Ali, but it was Rachel. "Sydney, thank goodness! Can you come over to the inn?"

"What's up, Rachel?"

"Well, I didn't really know who to call, because Glenn isn't around. At least, I can't find him. And someone should be here, it seems to me–"

"Rachel," I said firmly. "Take a deep breath. Tell me what's happened."

"It's the police," she said. "They just left. And they took him with them."

"Took who? What happened?"

"The manager. Mike. They've arrested him for Angela and Elizabeth Gonzalez's murders!"

15

So much for a quiet evening.

I thought about going to the police station, but I was quite sure that officialese would prevail and I wouldn't be able to see Mike. So I headed back to the Race Point, grateful that all the arguments over at Caroline's house had kept me from drinking too much. When I get together with my friends, I can sometimes overdo it.

Occasionally. Sometimes.

Brian was at the front desk and looked like his best friend had died. "Sydney!" he cried when I came in. "Oh, thank God! I don't know what to do!"

"Just do the front desk," I said. I was not having him cast me in a maternal comforting role. Besides, I wasn't old enough to be his mother, right?

Rachel was sitting alone in the parlor, clipboard next to her. I sat down on the other side of her. "What happened? I asked as quietly as I could. *Mike*? Not a chance. I'd known him for years. There was no way. But before I confronted the assembled branches of law enforcement, I needed to find out what was what. "Who arrested him?"

"The state police," she said. "That man— Henry Tibbets. He's a captain, or a general, or something." I was pretty sure they didn't have generals in the state police, but now wasn't the time to argue semantics. Besides, I'd been doing pretty much that all evening already.

"Okay," I said. "When did he come, and did he say anything about why?"

She shrugged. "I don't know. An hour ago, maybe? Everyone's already gone to the show."

"What show?"

She grabbed up her clipboard. "There's a dinner theater thing over at the Provincetown Theater," she said. "It's on the schedule. Everybody goes to it, usually."

"Except you."

A grimace. "I had to see to some of the details for the fashion show tomorrow night," she said. "I can't actually *attend* all the events, I just make sure they run smoothly."

"I get it. So everyone was out. And then?"

"And then that horrible man came in with two guys in uniform—and those are *awful* uniforms, Sydney, they looked like storm-troopers."

Well, she had that part right; for reasons best known to themselves, Massachusetts state police troopers wear a uniform that looks like a cross between a Luftwaffe pilot and a professional equestrian rider. "Okay. What happened then?"

"The fellow at reception asked if he could help. I was standing right there, Sydney, because I'd just been talking to him. What's his name? Brad?"

"Brian," I said.

"Brian. Right. So I was standing right there when they came in."

People react in different ways to shock. Another two minutes of this and I was sending out for brandy. "And what did they *say*, Rachel?"

"The horrible man asked for the manager. Well, no, he didn't exactly ask for the manager. He asked for Mike Pearson. And Brian said just a moment and he got him on the phone, and a minute later he came out of his office there."

"And?"

A deep breath. "And the horrible man said, Michael Pearson, I am arresting you for the murders of Robert Gonzalez and Elizabeth Gonzalez. You have the right to remain silent... And then he said that whole warning thing they do on *Law & Order*. You know the one. Miranda or Merrily or something. And then they left. And Brian tried to find the owner, but he called two different numbers and couldn't find him, and we just looked at each other because we didn't know what to do."

"Did Mike say anything? To anybody?"

She shook her head; her earrings jangled. "No, sweetie, not a word."

I sat back in my chair. "There's no way," I said. "He just *met* them. He'd have no reason in the world to wish either of them harm."

"So it had to be something else," she said.

"What do you mean?" What: some other reason Mike might have murdered someone?

"The reason they arrested him," she said.

"Yeah," I said grimly. "I guess I should go find out about that."

I went out to find Brian wailing on the phone to his boyfriend, which reminded me that at some point I should call mine, too. "Keep trying Glenn," I told him. What did one do now? Hire an attorney? I didn't know any attorneys. Post bail? Not from my checking account, I wasn't. Panic? Sure: that one was easy.

I called Julie's mobile. Voicemail. I left a message: "Don't even tell me that you guys are serious about Mike. Call me!"

She hadn't been the one to arrest him, of course. Which meant that chances were he was being transported to wherever the state police held criminals–no, strike that, where they held people who'd been wrongly accused and wrongly arrested. I tried Glenn again. Voicemail. I didn't leave any; I figured Brian had already been hysterical enough. Finally I called Ali. "Remember how your sister got something expedited for us last year?"

"I do," he said cautiously.

"Does she have any pull with the state police?" Come on, she was police commissioner for the whole city of Boston, that had to count for *something*.

"I doubt it," he said. "What's going on, Sydney?"

I took a deep breath. "They've arrested Mike," I said.

"What–for that murder? You've got to be kidding. *Mike?*"

"For both of them," I said. "For Angela and for Elizabeth, both. Glenn's nowhere to be found, and I don't even know where they've taken Mike, or what to do."

"Damn," he said, which for Ali was pretty much a shocking expletive. Ali likes Mike. A lot. It didn't matter if their friendship was inexplicable to me; it was very real to them. That was good: Ali would do something about it. If he could. "Where'd they take him?"

"I don't know. I just *said* that. I don't know where they take people, but I expect it's not our local police station."

"No," he said in agreement. He sounded distant, like he was doing sums in his head. "I'll call you back."

"Wait! No! Ali!" But he was gone.

Probably just as well. What I really needed from him right then was the boyfriend thing: reassuring, comforting, it'll-all-be-all-right-Sydney. And that wasn't the way to help Mike.

I took a deep breath. For now, I was on my own.

***

Julie still wasn't answering her mobile or returning the message I finally left for her at the police station, and I didn't know anyone else who could tell me what I needed to know. I closed my eyes and mentally roamed the streets of Provincetown, trying to visualize whether I knew anyone else who could help. At nearly nine at night.

Rachel disappeared on errands of her own, and Brian hovered nervously, going outside several times for a quick cigarette. I was just coming to the sorry conclusion that I was going to have to give it up for the night when Glenn walked in.

He'd probably never had such an effusive greeting.

Brian's eyes were sparkling. He's good at working reception, don't get me wrong; but he's very much into having a clearly defined path in front of him, preferably outlined by someone in authority, and doesn't respond well to changes in routine. A little like a toddler, or a cat. I spared a brief thought for Ibsen, who was surely ready for dinner by now.

Glenn looked exhausted. "They've got him in South Yarmouth," he said. "And no visiting until tomorrow."

"Visiting?" I looked at him in horror.

"Yeah, visiting. What?"

"It just sounds so–permanent," I said faintly.

Glenn shook his head. "Not if I can help it," he said. "Do you want a drink?" He didn't wait for an answer, led me into the Small Bar. A few people were there, none of them from the Fair; the play must still be happening up at the theater. Maryellen was behind the bar; she was at the last week of her summer season, leaving soon to go back to New York and acting school for the winter.

Glenn hoisted himself onto a barstool and pulled one out for me. "We have a lawyer," he said. "Hey, Maryellen."

"Hey, boss. Usual?"

"Several," he said. Maryellen looked at me. I shrugged. "I'll have the same thing."

"Coming up," she said, and started doing mysterious things behind the bar. I looked at Glenn. "Why did they arrest him?"

"No one's saying, but Margaret thinks it's fingerprint evidence."

"Who's Margaret?"

"Attorney."

We sat together in a gloom-laden silence until Maryellen came back with our drinks. I took a good-sized sip of mine and spluttered some of it out again, feeling my throat seize up. "What the hell *is* this?"

"Italian Manhattan," said Maryellen. "With a dash of something extra."

"A dash of what?"

"Secret."

Glenn had already started in on his. She'd put three cherries in it, and he ate one of them, quickly, putting the stem beside his glass before taking another hard swig. "And then there's the knife."

"What about the knife?" I said, knee-jerk reaction, and then stared at him. "Don't tell me it had Mike's fingerprints on it!"

"I don't know," Glenn said irritably. "I don't know what was on the knife. I only know that there are some fingerprints, some-where, and that some guest came forward and said they'd seen Mike with the knife. That evening. The evening Angela was stabbed."

"That's ridiculous," I protested. "How can anyone remember something like that? How could they know what that particular knife looked like? None of the guests ever sees Adrienne's knives. Before all this hap-pened, I couldn't even tell you what Adrienne's knives look like. I'll bet you couldn't, either. And, besides, Mike must have pocket knives, I don't know, letter openers…" In fact, as I thought about it, he had easy access to lots of different murderous instruments, had murder been his intent.

Glenn let my protests wind down. "Mike's been with us for fourteen years," he said heavily.

"And he'll be here for fourteen more!" I took a swig of the drink and this time didn't spit any out. "Listen, Glenn, he didn't do this."

"Of course he didn't."

"And besides…" Okay, Sherlock, *think*, don't just react. "What possible motive could he have? Seriously? Mike doesn't even know any of the Fair people, he told me so. Except for Rachel, of course. But besides that. You don't go around killing people you don't know."

"Of course not," said Glenn. "Two more," he said to Maryellen.

"I don't need another drink," I said.

"Of course you do. Two more, Maryellen."

"You got it, boss."

"And in case you thought that was bad enough, think again," Glenn said. "The press has finally gotten around to the tip of the Cape."

"As well they should," I said grimly. What did he expect? "Two murders, a botched shooting…"

"Whose side are you on, anyway?" He scowled at me and took a slug of the Manhattan. "They're sending people down from Boston. Two of 'em've already checked in."

"Surprised they could afford our rates," I murmured.

That got me a sharp look. "Sydney—"

I slid off my stool. Times like this…I like Glenn, don't get me wrong. He's a big, affable bear of a man who would do anything for people he loves. But even now, a year and a half after Barry's death, I still wish he were the one sitting there. I could talk to Barry in ways that I couldn't talk to anybody else, not even Ali. He would have known what to say. He would have known what to do. "I'm getting maudlin," I announced. "I'm going home."

He had already turned back to face the bar. Okay, fine, he wanted to play *Nighthawks*, not my problem. (Hopper lived on the Cape, did you know that?) "Will you let me know what happens tomorrow with Mike? If there's anything I can do."

He waved a hand in my direction and finished his second drink, reaching already for my untouched one. Glenn was well on the way to getting plastered.

Everybody reacts differently, I suppose.

16

Of course, I couldn't sleep.

I wished I'd headed over to Outer Cape Health when this all started: an Ambien prescription would have come in handy. But I hadn't, the alcohol was turning sour on me, and I kept thinking that there was something obvious I was missing.

Ibsen was disgruntled. Ibsen is in fact rarely if ever gruntled, but I'd woken him up when I arrived (my place isn't big enough for us to not always be in the same room), and my pacing was clearly annoying him. "Seriously," I said to him, "Mike's a smart guy. If he were going to kill someone with a knife, would he be flashing it around ahead of time for everyone to see?"

Ibsen yawned. "I know just what you mean," I told him. "There's just no way, is there? And then there's the whole motive thing. I really don't see it. He'd barely met Angela and Elizabeth. Actually, come to think of it, I can't imagine that he *did* meet them at all. He runs the place. He doesn't meet the guests."

Ibsen kept gazing at me. Waiting, no doubt, for me to come up with something clever. "I'm all out of cleverness," I said.

It was too late to call Ali or even Mirela. It was too late to do anything but go to bed. And I couldn't go to bed.

I sighed and pulled my laptop over and called up the Fantasia Fair website. Tomorrow was packed full of activities…another keynote speech, a poetry workshop, makeup and image consultations, a self-defense class, a book reading. Rehearsal for the fashion show, which I gathered was a major thing. And then the fashion show itself.

Dianne was coming over midafternoon to perform the renewal of vows ceremony for Megan and Sherry, which seemed to fit nicely between the keynote and the makeup class. I'd already had a conversation with the guys at Wildflower, and they were coming in the morning to decorate the trellis and gazebo, so that the patio would have an elegant and festive look–Jeff and John always did a fabulous job, that was one worry off my plate. I'd spoken to Martin about champagne and a small collation after the ceremony, and he'd presumably fixed it with Adrienne; I didn't go near her kitchen on a *good* day. I couldn't imagine what she'd be like with her favorite knife sitting in the evidence room in South Yarmouth. Or wherever it had landed.

I sighed and clicked on the fashion show. There were three categories: casual, formal, and fantasy, and first-timers were encouraged to take part. Would Angela have gone? What would she have borrowed for this momentous–

There it was.

That was what had been bothering me. Angela was wearing Coral's favorite dress and shoes. No matter why she was down on the beach alone–and that was a big question that I wasn't willing to put aside for too long–she was dressed like someone else, she was stabbed in the back (and everybody's back looks alike, right?), and *who would want to kill Coral?*

Slow down, Riley. Breathe. Think this through. It was night. Maybe the dress was irrelevant. Maybe it was too dark down there. Maybe it

189

was a crime of opportunity, or a hate crime, or…

I was getting carried away. I didn't even *know* how dark it got at the town beach next to the Johnson Street parking lot. That would be the first thing to check.

Well, it was dark out now.

No time like the present, I decided. If there wasn't enough light down there, then I'd know, and I wouldn't make a fool of myself to Julie and the guy from the state police and… "Gotta go out," I told Ibsen. He was sitting straight up, his tail wrapped nearly around his feet. He looked regal. He looked divine. There was a time when cats were gods, and Ibsen remembers.

I grabbed my leather jacket–might as well look cool, right?–and headed out. The Little Green Car turned over the first time, which I always took to be a good sign.

According to the dashboard clock, it was almost three. In the morning. Oh-dark-thirty. I should be asleep. I should have been asleep *hours* ago.

There were only a few other cars in the small parking lot. The parking kiosk was still working–free parking doesn't start until the beginning of November–but I guessed that people would be out to either move their cars or put in a payment before the parking enforcement people got up and about.

I pulled in to one of the spaces at the bottom of the lot, as close to the beach as I could. There was an outdoor light at the hammock shop, and a single tall streetlamp at the bottom of the lot.

There was no one around. No late-night drunks. No early dog-walkers. No insomniacs besides me. And absolutely no reason to be nervous.

Here's the thing. All the people from off-Cape, the tourists, even the second-home owners, they get out of their cars and they lock them. Immediately. Even if they're going to stand on front of said car in line at a friendly seafood take-out joint. Even if they're going to spend thirty seconds at an ATM. I get it: there are places where that makes sense. But not here. No one locks their cars—hell, most people I know don't lock their *houses*. And, don't tell anyone, but I used to be the Queen of Lost Keys, so every time I take mine out of the ignition, I stash them in the little storage bin on the dashboard. Always there. Seriously: the Little Green Car's the only thing I ever need the keys for.

So I pulled the keys out of the ignition and stashed them in the storage bin and got out of the car. My smartphone has a flash-light, but I didn't take it: the point of this exercise was to see what kind of ambient light was available here.

The car door slamming shut echoed off the buildings on either side of the parking lot. The harbor water was black, undulating, sensuous. I stepped down off the pavement onto the loose sand and kept walking. There was salt on the air, and the smell of seaweed, and something that I couldn't quite identify but that brought up a welling of nostalgia until I identified it: wood smoke. Someone had a fire going, even at three in the morning, against the sharp October night.

I shivered.

There were bright lights on MacMillan, lighting up the harbormaster's office and the fishing boats, with more lights behind them, over on Fisherman's Wharf. A couple of the boats had stark illumination from high up on their masts pointing down on their decks; I could imagine that was useful for unloading fish. Or maybe even loading and icing them; like a lot of other people, everything I know about professional fishing I know from *The Perfect Storm*, written by the inn's sometime neighbor on Commercial Street, Sebastian Junger. Okay, so I'm not above name-dropping. The point being that there were screaming bright lights on the boats and I had no idea why, and that was that.

And there were lights at the bottom of Johnson Street, and outdoor lights from the hammock shop, and even a couple of more feeble ones from condo associations that backed up onto the beach. The restaurants—Pepe's and the Harbor Lounge—were dark, which made some sense given the time. But as it turned out, I didn't need them.

I stood there, still, breathing deeply. This was where Angela was attacked, where someone had come up behind her and hadn't minded getting bloody, hadn't minded the thought of blood and the feeling of a knife going into flesh. I found myself closing my fingers around an imaginary one. It wasn't even easy, I thought: I've cut up raw chickens, and it's a lot harder to do than when they've already been roasted. You have to really want it. Maybe you have to really need it.

My fingers were starting to cramp. I stretched them, shook out my arm. There were a lot of shadows, deceptive, indistinct. There was a rowboat pulled up past the high-water mark and it blended seamlessly with the dried seaweed, dark blurry shapes at the edge of my vision. Had Angela seen someone coming at her in the last moments just like that, blurred and indistinct, at the edge of her sight? Probably not; she would have fought.

I kept forgetting that she was a cop.

A sudden wind whipped on off the water, snarling my hair. I wrapped myself tighter in the leather jacket. Angela was a cop. Trained. I didn't know that much about police training, but I knew what I saw with Julie: she never ever stopped observing. It never got turned off. We went into Chach's for breakfast, she'd be talking and laughing and the whole time her eyes were going, recording, seeing. She'd be able to tell you how many people were at each table, their genders, possibly even the food they were eating. She'd know who felt uncomfortable. She'd know who had a secret. And she'd never miss a beat in our conversation.

Me? If I registered what the *waiter* was wearing, I was batting a thousand.

Angela had been trained like that. Angela knew what lurked in the periphery. Angela would have heard someone approaching her in the sand, felt it, known it somehow with the part of her that never stopped being a cop, ever.

And she hadn't turned, and she hadn't fought back. She hadn't even run.

It was inexplicable.

I shivered again and reluctantly took off the jacket and then the red pajama top that was underneath. Shaking now, I put the jacket back on, jamming my arms into the sleeves, the leather cold against my skin. And tossed the pajama top over into the sand where they'd found Angela. And took a deep breath.

Okay. You could see colors. Red especially. Mystery solved.

Anyone would see that the person walking here, even in the dark, was wearing red. There was enough light for even the least-keen observer (i.e., *moi*) to tell. So unless it was random (pretty much ruled out), or someone knew for sure that Angela would be wearing Sherry's favorite outfit on the first night of the Fair, I thought it might be a good idea to look at a different motive altogether.

And maybe give Coral a little protection in the meantime. Because there was no guarantee that whoever had wanted her dead in the first place had given up the plan. I had a feeling that murderers weren't that easily diverted. "Oh, you know, I meant to kill him, but it just got so difficult that I decided to have my nails done instead." You have to really, really have a good reason to not just want someone dead but to be willing to do it the

DIY way; that kind of resolution, if anything, deepens when faced with adversity.

Anyway, I'd figured out what I'd needed to figure out. I grabbed my pajama top, stuffed it into my jacket (no way was I taking that this off again), and got back in my Honda. Heated seats. I love the Little Green Car.

And that time, when I drank my warm milk and slipped under the comforter, I went straight off to sleep.

***

The Race Point Inn was abuzz. There was no other word for it. The air was practically fizzing with excitement. "Fashion show tonight!" one person, dressed in a whole lot of brightly colored scarves, called to me as soon as I got in the door. "There's still time to register!"

I looked down at myself in case by some strange sleepwalking twist I'd attired myself in anything that looked even remotely fashionable. Nope. A black dress I'd chosen because it was easy to pull on over my head and then leave alone, grey tights, black flats. Red hair tamed. Mascara. I looked like a nun from a more progressive sort of convent.

Hey, on three hours' sleep, you don't get grooming, okay?

I staggered into the breakfast room and poured coffee. Glenn was there, eating and looking at the newspaper and talking on the phone, all at the same time. I slumped down at the table beside him, took a swallow of coffee, and surveyed the room. Fantasia Fair guests, most of them; but there were a couple of tables taken up by serious people with all sorts of boxes and equipment, talking earnestly and simultaneously into phones. The media had arrived. And, like it or not, that was part of the fizziness.

Rachel alighted on my other side. "So I'll start by saying how terrible it is that they're here for the reason they're here," she said in a rush. "But they're covering the fashion show tonight! Imagine!"

"Imagine," I echoed and buried my face in my coffee again. Glenn got off the phone. "Once you wake up, I want you on reception," he said to me.

"Why me?"

"Because you're one of the few grownups in this place."

"Brian's a grownup."

"Brian's out posing by the pool for some crap newsmagazine," said Glenn. "And Richard's supposed to be on the desk, but I'm giving him to Rachel to help set up for the fashion show tonight. He and Martin can handle that between them."

"Any news?" I asked.

He shook his head. He was becoming a very shaggy bear indeed. "Not yet. Margaret says she'll call me."

"Margaret?" Rachel echoed.

"Attorney."

"Oh, that's right!" Rachel had clearly forgotten her panic of the night before. "They arrested Mike, didn't they?"

Glenn grunted. I drank some more coffee.

"Well, of course they'll let him go," said Rachel. "He didn't do it. I don't think he's even come out of his office more than a couple of times since we've been here."

"He's a behind-the-scenes kind of guy," I agreed.

"So he couldn't have hated Angela. You don't hate somebody you don't know," she said.

I shrugged. "I hate the president," I said.

"You know *about* him," she said. "That's different."

Glenn looked at me pointedly. I sighed and got up. "I'm off to reception, then," I said. "Good," he answered.

I refilled my cup and made it over to the front desk without mishap. There was already a line waiting.

"Where do we sign up for the fashion show?"

"Do we have to go to the rehearsal?"

"What if we have an extra little act we want to slip in?"

"What time is the makeup class? Lord, I need it!"

"You said it, not me!"

I looked at them in horror. I didn't know any of the answers, and there was a headache building, and I felt a little underwater. I was going to get that Ambien prescription if it killed me, because not having it was doing a number on my functioning.

"Rachel knows," I said, pointing in the direction of the breakfast room. "She's in there. So's the inn's owner. They can tell you."

That cleared them out nicely, and I didn't even feel a shred of remorse. Glenn and Rachel could handle themselves. Glenn and Rachel had had a full night's sleep.

I'd been anxious to take my half-articulated and half-remembered thoughts from the night before and shake them out a little in the cold light of day, but my brain wasn't particularly cooperating. A couple of guests checked in. A few media types stopped by and asked for directions to the police station, and why there was a monument on the hill, and when the district attorney was going to make a statement.

Mostly I stood there and leaned on the desk and eavesdropped into people's conversations. We have a large foyer–well, large by Provincetown standards–and there were plenty of people coming and going. I flogged my last issue of Provincetown Magazine, agreed that there seemed to be a cold front moving in, called in a reservation for a whale watch. I could have done all of it in my sleep.

All right, I'm pretty sure that I *did* do all of it in my sleep.

But underneath it all was the thread I'd caught hold of last night and was holding for dear life. The killer hadn't meant to kill Angela. They'd meant to kill Coral. They'd probably only killed Elizabeth because she'd figured that out. It was all ridiculously clear once you realized about the dress...and saw that you absolutely, positively couldn't have mistaken it for anything else down on the Johnson Street beach.

The real problem was that I had a brilliant new theory and absolutely no one with whom to share it. What would Nancy Drew do?

I waved cheerfully to people I vaguely recognized, answered a few more inane questions, and then Megan and Sherry, another couple in tow, showed up. I swallowed hard. This wasn't exactly what I'd had in mind, public place, hey, Sherry, Megan, anyone want your friend Coral dead? How do you segue neatly into that?

"We just came by to firm up plans for this afternoon," said Sherry. "Oh, don't you know each other? Sorry! We always just assume, we've all been coming to the Fair for so long, you know? These are our dear friends Marti and Dezz. Girls, this is Sydney, she's just marvelous, and she's arranged the ceremony for us today."

"This is a great hotel," Dezz told me. "I think the Fair's found the perfect home." *Well, maybe, except for the fact that this inn attracts death like I attract sunburn. Shut up, Riley.*

"So Dianne's going to be here about fifteen minutes early, just to chat with you," I said. And the guys from Wildflower have probably finished already–they're the ones that are marvelous, not me. All I do is get fantastic people together." I smiled. "What are you wearing?"

They giggled together. "Our same wedding gowns!" said Sherry. "The ones we wore when we got married."

"Well, not quite. When we *first* got married, Sherry identified as a man," Megan told me. "But then, later…well, we had a second wedding. Not legal or official or anything, but just something for us, and Sherry made a gown for it."

"Fabulous," Dezz said. "We should do it sometime, too, Marti."

"We've been married way too long," Marti said. "I'll never fit back into my wedding gown! Not even in my dreams."

"That makes it a perfect excuse to buy a new one," Megan said, smiling.

I didn't know how to ask what I wanted to know, so I just plunged in. "Are Taisie and Coral around?" I made it as casual sounding as I could. "I thought you might be together; I mean, you all seem close."

Megan shrugged. "Well, on and off," she said. "We only ever see them here at Fantasia Fair. And, besides…well, here's the thing, they go through good times and bad times."

"Like any couple," said Dezz quickly.

Megan glanced at her. "Yeah, well, sometimes with them it's more uncomfortable," she said. "There are silences, you know, really frigid ones, and you know how it is, you feel embarrassed. You never really know how to behave around people when they're doing that. There's nowhere to look." I thought that was pretty observant of her.

"They shouldn't be doing that in a public place," Dezz said. Dezz apparently had some very clear standards and even clearer opinions.

"Well, people do, don't they," said Megan. Nothing ruffled her. "Anyway, we're here to talk about this afternoon! Tell me again: when do we meet with Dianne? I know you just told us, I'm so excited, I can't remember anything."

"She'll be here early to chat with you before the ceremony. I'll bring her to your room, if you'd like." I knew they were planning something of an entrance to the patio area, and I didn't want to spoil that by having them meet with her out in one of the inn's public areas. "And I'll have everything ready for you by then, too. Are you re-exchanging your rings?"

"Well," said Sherry, "we were, except that then we thought, hell, no, let's make it all new."

"So we went yesterday and bought some rings in town," said Megan.

"We wanted to go to Ruby's, but they're gone now," said Sherry.

"I know," I agreed. Everyone was unhappy about Ruby's owners choosing to retire. For decades it had been the go-to place for fine jewelry on Commercial Street. For some visitors, a summer wasn't complete without at least one purchase from Ruby's.

"But we have lovely ones anyway," said Megan. "So we're really doing it all over again."

"And it looks like the photographer's going to have some competition," said Sherry. "Seriously. All this media! Everyone looks thoroughly confused, don't they?"

It was true; the reporters might have been drooling over the "if it bleeds, it leads" headlines they could get from a double murder, but for sure they hadn't been expecting anything like Fantasia Fair. Not even a little bit. I wondered if they'd bother to educate themselves, or just use it as another excuse for behaving like visitors to a zoo—and writing their stories that way. I'd apparently become singularly protective of Fair-goers.

"So we'll see you this afternoon," Megan was saying. "I'm so excited!"

"Yeah, let's go, I think we're running late," Dezz said. Dezz was the sort of person, I thought, who would always be the one to point out that sort of thing.

I waited until they were out of earshot, and in fact looked around to make sure that nobody else could hear me, before pulling out my phone and hitting Julie's icon. Be there, I prayed silently. Be there, be there, be...

"What is it, Sydney?"

"Hey, Julie." I hadn't *really* expected her to pick up. "Listen, this may be nothing, or it may be important, I don't know."

"What?"

I took a breath. "I think you should have someone watching Coral," I said. I couldn't remember her last name for the life of me. "I think she's in some danger."

"And why exactly is that?"

I hoped I'd never run afoul of the law and have Julie interrogate me. Even this conversation made me feel guilty. "Julie, I think that it was Coral who was supposed to be the victim. Angela was wearing her dress when she got killed. Her *favorite* dress. And it was really unmistakable, bright red, all that chiffon, you know? And you could see it in the dark. The color, I mean. I went down to the Johnson Street beach last night–"

"You did *what*?"

"–and there's that one streetlamp, but it's enough, you can make out colors. And anyone walking that way, under the Harbor Lounge walkway, they'd be silhouetted against the lights from the pier. So you couldn't see who it was, but you could sure see that dress." The next part was going to sound ridiculous, me telling a detective how to do her job, but in for a penny, in for a pound. "And if they wanted Coral dead then, they probably still want her dead now, right?"

"You went down to the beach in the middle of the night to figure this out?"

"I couldn't sleep," I said.

"That insomnia's getting you into trouble," said Julie.

"For sure," I agreed. But I'm not wrong, am I?"

There was a pause. "You're not wrong," she said.

I let out my breath; I hadn't realized I'd been holding it. "So what's going to happen?" I asked. "Are you putting someone there to keep an eye on her?"

"You forget that the state police have already made an arrest," she said. "They're not interested in any other theory of the crime right now. And I'm off the case. They're the only ones investigating. They work for the DA's office; I just work for the residents of Provincetown." She paused. "And they've arrested Mike," she said. "End of story."

Mike. I felt guilty that I hadn't been thinking about him. It was a good thing that he had

Glenn on his side, since I clearly wasn't being of much help. "But he didn't do it."

"That's a persuasive argument, Sydney, but unfortunately it's not going to be enough for my colleagues," she said.

"I could live without the sarcasm."

"And I could live without you telling me my job," she said, unexpectedly. Julie is usually unflappable. Something was getting under her skin, and it wasn't me, we hadn't been talking long enough for me to really annoy her yet. What it meant, I thought, was that the Staties had frozen her out of the investigation. "Where are you, anyway?" I asked.

"I'm in Provincetown," she said. "I'm part of the Provincetown police department, remember?"

Ouch. I'd gotten it right. "So can't you do anything about protecting Coral?"

"The best thing for Coral," she said, "is for her to not be alone. There's a lot going on there, just make sure she does all the activities."

"Me?"

"Who else? You're concerned; do something about it." Her voice softened. "Listen, chances are she's safe. Whoever did this doesn't want to get caught. Angela and Elizabeth were both alone when they were attacked. She has a wife, right?"

"Right."

"So between you and the wife and the schedule of events, you should be able to keep an eye on her. At least until they figure out they have the wrong person in custody."

"And what about you?" I demanded. "What are you doing?"

"Police work," she said obscurely. "What I should have been doing from the beginning. See ya, Sydney."

There was something else that was poking around the margins of my brain. Something ominous, like the first twinge of a toothache, when you know that it's inevitably the beginning of something painful and protracted if you ignore it. Usually you choose to ignore it anyway, and things do get much worse.

Whatever this message was, I didn't want to ignore it. But how could I manage that when I didn't even know what it was?

17

Brian finally arrived at noon to relieve me. "What a trip!" he exclaimed. He seemed energized and alert, neither of which I particularly felt.

"What do you mean?" I asked sourly, though I knew what he meant.

"The cameras! And the reporters! And everything."

"Giving out interviews? Is that what you've been up to all morning?"

"Well, it's not like Glenn or Mike were around," he said a little defensively. "Someone had to talk to them."

"And you're third in command around here?"

He looked at me sharply. "You seem re-markably peevish," he said.

Did he actually say peevish? "That's funny," I said, "because I *feel* remarkably peevish. It's a matching set."

He waved an arm. "So go," he said. "Go do…whatever it is that you do."

"Gladly." Why was I being so nasty? I hate it when your emotions take hold of you and you can't seem to change them. I didn't even have the excuse of having my period, which is when I usually get over-emotional. None of my mood was Brian's fault, and yet here I was, ready to take him on. It was ridic-ulous.

Instead, I decided to track down Coral and Taisie. If Julie thought it was worth keep-ing an eye on them, then keep an eye was ex-actly what I would do. It was lunchtime, and they could be anywhere in town, but there was a better-than-average chance that they were here, because Wednesday's lunch, the schedule had informed me, was a ticketed af-fair here at the inn.

It turned out to be a buffet, and I saw Coral right away, picking up a plate from one end of the line.

Right. So you can see her. And that helps ex-actly–how? If someone were to rush up to her with a knife right now, you think there's anything you could do about it? Got any fancy ninja moves to show off?

I paused by the maître d' station and Martin turned to greet me. "You're not here for lunch, are you?"

"Why, is it bad?"

He grimaced. "Adrienne doesn't believe in buffets. If it's not made to order, then she's not making it," he said.

"Tell me again why she works here."

He shrugged. "Because she's a brilliant chef, Sydney, no way around that."

"So who's doing the buffet?"

"Lunch cooks. Under protest." Quite apart from the inn itself, our restaurant has five stars, and buffets do not five stars maintain.

"They'll survive," I said without thinking.

"They will," he agreed. "Have you heard anything from Glenn?"

I shook my head. "I keep checking my phone."

"As do I," he said somberly. Even his moustache seemed deflated.

We stood there together in a gloomy silence for a while. I kept my eyes on Coral and Taisie, sitting now at a table with a group of other people, while trying to look casual. I wasn't altogether sure I was pulling it off.

Martin wasn't fooled. "Why are you watching them?" he asked.

"What? Who?"

"That table over there. What's going on?"

It wasn't like Julie had asked me to keep it a secret, I thought. "I think that Coral—that woman in the yellow dress?—was supposed to get killed Sunday night, not Angela." I picked at the corner of one of the menus and he slapped my hand gently away. "Angela came here with no clothes. Well, you know what I mean, no *women's* clothes. Didn't know where to buy them. And couldn't buy them at home."

"I heard he was a cop," Martin said.

I nodded. The pronoun was correct, in this case: when Angela had been home, Angela had definitely been a *he*. "So anyway, when they arrived on Sunday, Angela didn't have any clothes to wear. Rachel waved her off, but they're all so nice, you know, they all gave her something. In fact, what Coral said was that everyone gave Angela their *favorite* outfit, so she'd feel great. And Coral's favorite dress was what she was wearing when she was killed."

Martin stirred. "Why?"

"Why, what? Maybe because she liked it the most of the ones she got. Maybe it was the first one she got. Who knows why?"

He shook his head. "Not what I meant," he said. "Why would someone want to kill– Coral, is that her name?"

I stared at him. Of course I hadn't thought it that far through. "I don't know," I said. "I don't really know anything about her."

"Maybe," Martin said, "you should."

***

Five minutes later I was on the phone with Ali. Who wasn't happy. Not even a little bit. "What do you mean, you went down to check out the beach? At what time?"

"Three o'clock," I mumbled. "Something around that."

"Are you completely insane? Someone in Provincetown's already killed two people and you think it's a nice night for a stroll?"

"I drove," I said defensively. "I had to see something."

"At three o'clock in the morning."

"Well, I couldn't sleep anyway, and that's when it occurred to me."

There was a silence on the other end of the line. "You're an idiot," he finally said.

"Maybe," I conceded.

"Definitely," my beloved said. "Definitely an idiot." He sighed.

"And the dashing ICE agent hasn't ever done anything remotely dangerous," I said.

"I'm a trained professional," he said. "You're not supposed to attempt this at home."

I sighed. He was right, of course, if you looked at it that way. The thing is, random violence doesn't just happen. Not here; or, at least, not for a long time. Back in the 60s or 70s—the days of hitchhiking—there was a guy who murdered some women on the Outer Cape and buried them in Truro. Later a socialite called Christa Worthington had been killed in her home in Truro in the 1990s, and she knew her killer, or at least the guy convicted of her murder.

And that was pretty much it.

Besides, I read my share of both newspapers and murder mysteries, and it does seem that motive plays a fairly major part in deciding to kill somebody. Sociopaths and psychopaths aside, with some famous exceptions, humans don't seem to kill each other randomly. There's usually a reason. Some encounter, at the very least, something that made the other person into an obstacle, something that had to be removed.

Even Colonel Mustard in the library with a candlestick needed a motive.

I tried to remember, again, the conversation I'd had with Julie about whether or not killers slept well at night. They didn't see other people the way most of us do, she'd said. Other people weren't really people: they had *functions* in the would-be killer's life. They could help the killer reach their goals, or they could stand in the killer's way.

And it was often the one standing in the killer's way who got another descriptor after their name: victim.

I wasn't standing in anybody's way to anything. I didn't have a fortune, or even a will. I hadn't seen or heard anything compromising to anybody. In fact, much as I didn't like admitting it, I was one of the most innocuous people on the face of the earth.

I said so to Ali. "No one wants me dead."

"Don't tempt me." The humor was returning to his voice. "Just promise you'll keep your insomnia indoors, at least for the moment," he said.

"Promise," I said promptly. Best to reassure him. Besides, tonight at least, I was sleeping. Please God. "So."

"So?"

"You did call me," I pointed out. "Presumably for a reason. The last thing I remember, you were going to see if you could apply pressure to your sister who might in turn apply pressure to—"

"All right, all right," he said. "I won't even point out that I might be calling you because I happen to like you."

"Not your style."

"Not my style," he agreed. "Anyway, once I heard about Mike, I really got into it."

"And you hadn't been before? Not for me? Not because I asked you?"

"*You* weren't arrested," he said reasonably.

"Fair enough," I agreed. "Go on."

"So they've got a witness says she saw him with the knife on Sunday evening, sometime after it was stolen. They're not saying who, but that's normal: police procedure isn't to share names too much."

"No. Normal police procedure is to arrest someone on anybody's say-so," I snapped.

"It's one of the inn's guests, someone there for Fantasia Fair," he said, unaffected. "But that wouldn't be enough for an arrest. Questioning, maybe; not an arrest."

"So what else do they have?"

"Apparently his fingerprints were also on the knife," Ali said. "And on a glass by the bedside."

I didn't say anything. This was sheer lunacy, I was thinking. Mike would have had no reason to be in their room–okay, that was a given. But if he had gone there, there must have been one. One I didn't see. One he hadn't even let his best buddy Ali see. "Has he talked to his attorney?" I asked. "Has he talked to Glenn? Did he say why they're there?"

"I don't know," said Ali. "You have to understand, there's just so much interagency cooperation will get you, and I don't have any official standing here."

"Your sister…"

"My sister," he said firmly, "is extended some courtesies by the state police. That doesn't mean they take her into their confidence. There's just so far either of us can push it. You'd do better trying to get information from your district attorney. It's his office determines charges."

"I don't know the district attorney," I said. "I know you." There was an edge to my voice, and I could feel something burning in the back of my throat. I really wished Ali were here and not there. Wherever *there* was.

"One thing," he said, "from the medical examiner. You know they saw them right away." Yeah; that made sense. Most of the Cape's casualties are opioid overdoes or traffic accidents. Homicide would get priority. "And the knife wounds, there were three of them, they definitely indicated a shorter person. The angle of the blade into the soft tissue."

"That doesn't help," I said miserably; Mike's not much taller than I am, and I'm five foot seven. Next to most of the participants, excluding significant others, he would be short.

"No, but this might. Elizabeth was strangled by someone who sat on top of her while she was lying flat on the bed. They broke a couple of her ribs. The bruising patterns on her neck indicate a fairly small hand. They told me the measurements, but I didn't write it down and I can't remember. But it was someone with small hands."

"What do Mike's hands look like?"

"As to that," Ali said, "I couldn't hazard a guess."

I shut my eyes and tried to visualize, but it's just not something that you notice, is it? The shape and size of someone's hands? "We'd have noticed if they were particularly small, wouldn't we?" I said doubtfully.

"You'd think, wouldn't you?"

"Anyway, we have an advantage. *We* know that it wasn't Mike. *They* don't. So it's up to us to figure out who it was." I was visualizing myself running around the Fair events, squinting at the size of people's hands. I wondered how long I could keep that up before they carted me away to the nice place with padded walls and men in white jackets.

"Hang on a minute, there, Nancy Drew," said Ali. "Who's this *we?*"

"Okay, me, then. *I* have to figure it out."

"No, you're not. You're going to let the professionals handle this."

"What professionals?" I demanded. "Julie's been…I don't know the word. Disenfranchised? The state police want this one all to themselves."

"Of course they do. That's the way it works," said Ali. "It's not that they want it: it's that they've *got* it. Once there's a homicide, it's the district attorney's case, and the state police are the investigative arm of the district attorney. And, listen, they know what they're doing." He paused. "And they're the ones who should be doing it. Listen to me. They're professionals. They solve crimes for a living."

"Last year, I—"

"Last year you were damned *lucky*. And don't think for a moment that I don't know how lucky we both were. I'm serious, Sydney. Don't ask too many questions." He took a deep breath. "People get scared when you ask too many questions," he said.

"Better I should ask them than Julie should, or the guy from the state police!" I exclaimed. I couldn't remember his name. "If I'm asking, it's just nosiness. If they're asking, it's threatening."

"He's a cop, for Pete's sake!" Even at his most upset, Ali doesn't swear. Well, that's not quite true: he just swears *differently*. He doesn't take the name of God–Allah–in vain, anyway. "Listen to me: This guy has killed two people already. And that's all you'd be to them: another person. Another person who might be getting close to the truth. Cops aren't people, not in that sense. Someone would think twice before killing a cop."

"Oh, yeah, like they thought twice when they killed Angela."

"If your theory is right, they didn't know she was a cop. You can't have it both ways."

Well, there was that. I counted to three, then did it again. *Breathe, Riley.* "All right," I said.

"All right?" He sounded suspicious.

"All right. I won't ask probing questions. I won't measure hand spans."

But maybe, just maybe, I could get someone else to do it for me.

18

For most of us, life went on, and the next thing on my agenda was professional: the renewal of vows ceremony for Megan and Sherry. Wildflower had outdone themselves with the bower and had added centerpieces to the tables that encircled it; Martin had done his part with tablecloths, crystal, and silver. There was to be champagne and some light hors-d'oeuvres, along with oysters that Mike had brought before he…*deep breath, Riley, don't go there*. Mike's relaxation was oystering; he had a very small aquaculture grant in the harbor, not far from the breakwater. *Don't think about Mike now*. "We'll need lemons and horseradish and—"

"Don't worry," Martin said. "I'll get Greta to put everything out."

"You're the best," I assured him.

The brides withdrew, giggling, to their room, and I headed home myself to change. The almost-sleepless night was catching up to me, and I needed a shower and an espresso, in that order, to feel halfway human again. Besides, you can't detect when you're half asleep.

Ibsen greeted me with a sharp accusatory cry and led me to his empty bowl. Had I seriously forgotten to feed him this morning? Or was he counting on my tiredness to get a second helping? With Ibsen, you never knew. I cracked open a can of cat food and dumped it into the dish, then headed into the shower.

The one really amazing thing about my apartment is the water pressure. I love it. I could stand under a shower for hours. It was like getting a massage every time.

Midway through I found myself crying. And I didn't even know why. Just tired, and stressed, and it was hitting me all over again that two people I'd known, even if not particularly well, had died violently over the past four days. There was a more-than-decent chance that it could still happen to someone else. And my friend and colleague had been arrested for it. I felt like I was living in some bizarre alternate reality where nothing was as it seemed. Alice through the looking-glass time.

I sobbed for a while and then gradually the tears subsided and petered off on their own, and then I scrubbed myself so hard my skin was red and rough when I finally got out. Still a long ways to go before I could go to bed, I thought, looking longingly at it. Right now all I wanted was to curl up under my comforter and be done with it all.

Have you ever noticed, when you're over-tired, nothing is quite right? It's as if inanimate objects have one sole intent, and that's to thwart you. I looked through my closet three times (don't misunderstand, it's not that extensive a collection, it's just that I was moving particularly slowly) before I decided on something that would look appropriate: the purple dress that qualified as one of my two party dresses, with black lace at the neck and hem. Another dress I had to zip up, naturally; but this one, blessedly, had the zipper on the side, so I kept my contortions to a minimum. This was why people kept lady's maids, I decided. Forget the rest of the duties: just zip me in (and out) of my clothing as necessary. Tights, shoes, and a quick five minutes with the blow-drier before I just put a headband in my hair and left it at that. What you see is what you get.

I walked all the way back to the inn. There wasn't anywhere to park and I didn't feel like risking the necessary balance on my bicycle. Not in this dress.

By the time I got there, people were starting to drift onto the patio. There's an outside bar, opened when there's an event, and Gus was happily mixing drinks and pouring wine. I sat on one of the barstools and turned to survey my domain. He followed my gaze. "It looks nice," he offered.

"It does," I agreed. "I work with great people. And it looks like the guests are having a good time."

He was shaking a martini. "Everybody's jazzed for the fashion show tonight."

I nodded. There was definitely something in the air, fizzing like a fuse lit on a wire, something electric. I couldn't get hold of it, somehow, couldn't interpret what I was feeling. It was a little like the way the air feels just before a storm: anticipatory, slightly off, dangerous and mysterious. A sound, almost, the air shimmering and humming like… and then I had it. When I first came to Provincetown, I went on a self-guided tour of every art gallery I could find. I loved the way one of the artists caught the flat lines of dunes and water and sky. He offered to show me his work-space upstairs from the gallery, filled with Buddhas and prayer beads and his images of the sea, stretching out into the horizon. He made me hold a bowl with my fingertips and moved a brush around it, the sound clear in the dusty air. *You have a strong presence*, he told me. *You're at peace with yourself.*

This air felt like the sound that came from that bowl. This air felt like a message was go-ing round and round, but only those who could decipher its secret language could un-derstand it. The vibration of something real and present and indefinable. Maybe Bud-dhists would understand it. I didn't, and it was spooking me.

Dianne arrived, dressed in her white cas-sock and rainbow stole. "Nice crowd," she commented, looking around. I nodded. "It's something to celebrate, a relationship like this," I said. "There's a lot out there to tear people apart, more for these people than for anybody else."

I kept that thought going as I watched her take her place under the arbor and cue the music. If weddings themselves were brave and filled with hope and trust and maybe even a little magic, then something like this had to be even more courageous. Because the people already know what's involved, they've been living it, day in and day out—and they know how cold and unforgiving the world around them can be, too.

Pushing the edge of the envelope always seemed to come out in personal relationships, didn't it? The first open interracial couples, the first open gay couples, and now trans couples who cared more about happiness than about assessing where someone happened to locate them on a generic gender-based pie chart.

It felt good to be part of something like this, one of those times when you actually know that you're doing something important. If it weren't for that tightness in the air, that vibration, that sense of impending…something. Not doom, I told myself. Everyone here seemed happy, supportive, kind. I was the only one bringing negative thoughts to the table. Maybe I was just creating my own fears.

And then the two brides were walking in, hand in hand, wearing frothy white dresses ("we're wearing them for the fashion show, too, might as well get the mileage out of them," Megan had told me) and looking every bit as happy as anyone I'd ever seen, and I decided that I was just imagining things. That can happen when you haven't had enough sleep. And when people close to you have been murdered.

We're gathered here today to reaffirm the love that Sherry and Megan have for each other, and the companionship which they have chosen...

My mind wandered away from the words as I looked around at the people on the patio— fifty or sixty of them, some holding cocktail glasses, a few holding hands. I knew a whole lot of the guests by name now, and easily (and quickly) identified Coral and Taisie, because I was still unconvinced that Coral was completely safe, even in a crowd. Lisa. Evelyn. Rachel Parsons, without her clipboard for once, looking around at everybody but the couple; she had something on her mind. Dee-Dee. Teresa. Thanks to my unexpected and extended shifts at the front desk, I knew everybody there by sight at least, and no one, not a single one of them, looked like a murderer.

Still, there was a good chance that someone was.

I shivered; the humming seemed more taut, more real. I couldn't believe that nobody else was sensing it.

This is a love that has seen them through joys and sorrows alike, through the good times and the bad times, through fear and gratitude and uncertainty, and that continues to be a source of strength and inspiration...

"They're amazingly strong," murmured a voice beside me and Mirela slid onto the barstool next to mine.

"I know," I murmured back. "To have gone through what they have to, in their everyday lives, and still have this much joy."

"I didn't mean that." She was impatient. "To be here despite the murders, sunshine. Anyone else would have gone home."

I forget that, for Mirela, everything is personal. "Right now, you're the only one thinking about that," I said. Which was a lie, of course: I was, too.

She turned so she could face me, the better to hiss in my ear. "I have been reading," she said. "Did you know that trauma inflicted by other people, when it is done on purpose, is more difficult to come to terms with than the worst of all natural disasters?"

"No," I whispered back. "There might be another better time you could tell me about it."

She ignored that. "Acts of violence are also harder to process than accidents," she said. She sounded like she was quoting someone. She probably was. On top of all her other assets, Mirela has an eidetic memory. She'd be easy to hate. "It is experienced as an attack on human integrity, sunshine. So then there's just increasing anger, loss of trust in people, and, in fact, a lot greater chance of going completely crazy. So none of them, really, should be this cheerful."

The reading Sherry and Megan have selected for their recommitment ceremony is titled "On Marriage," by Kahlil Gibran. The words talk about the intense melding of two people in marriage...and at the same time, about two people who maintain an intense separateness...a separateness that keeps their individuality intact and flourishing. It's a lovely conundrum...and perhaps a formula for a successful marriage. The reader is Candace Mancuso.

I hissed at Mirela, "Can you keep your armchair psychology to yourself for five more minutes, do you think?"

"I thought you would be happy, that I am helping you to solve this crime," she said.

"I'd be happier if you didn't have to do it in the middle of a wedding."

"But what if the murderer is here?"

"You really think that telling me how people process grief and fear is going to help pinpoint who it is? Like there'll be a neon light flashing over his head?"

"Not his head," said Mirela. "Hers."

Wedding rings are a symbol of commitment and love. The rings are circular, like their love, with no beginning and no end. They represent what has been, and what will always be. They are made of solid, sturdy material, material that's meant to survive years and years of hand-holding, washing dishes, swimming, arguments, and tender caresses. Couples wear their wedding rings every day as a symbol of their love.

Of course. Ali had said that the hand-span around Elizabeth's neck was small, which pretty much eliminated anyone whose gender at birth had been male. I stared down for a moment at my own hands. "You got it, sunshine," whispered Mirela. "It has to be a woman!" She sounded triumphant, like she'd cracked the case.

I looked back up at the guests. There were only three trans men who were there, and probably about eighteen or twenty cis women, partners or wives of the Fantasia Fair attendees. That narrowed the smaller-hand possibilities at a truly alarming rate.

The institution of marriage has inspired many cultural icons to express what they think it takes for a marriage to be successful. Their words can be an

*inspiration to others. Now I'll ask Sherry and Me-
gan's friends to come forward and share a few quota-
tions about marriage to encourage and inspire the two
brides today. Some of these words are filled with wis-
dom, and some with humor. Some have the ring of
seasoned experience, some have a surprise twist, while
some simply express the obvious.*

There was general movement as a few
people sorted themselves out from the crowd
and went forward, clutching index cards or
pieces of paper, one or two of them looking
awkward and anxious. You see all sorts at a
wedding. Someone I didn't know started to
read, and I turned back to Mirela. "So who?"
I whispered.

"I am not the detective here."

"There is no detective here," I snapped.
Julie was MIA. Henry, the guy from the state
police, ditto.

"Perhaps you are not one, but you act like
it sometimes."

"You're not being helpful."

I turned away and scanned the guests
again. Rachel had moved; she was on the periphery now, and apparently doing the same
thing I was, although with somewhat less of
a vantage point. I wondered what she was
thinking. I wondered how much it was cost-
ing her emotionally to keep all of this together

and moving forward when everything seemed to be conspiring to drag the whole enterprise down.

The readings were over and Megan and Sherry went up to the front and turned to face the guests. "We mostly want to thank all of you," said Sherry, and there was raw emotion in her voice. She stopped and swallowed hard. "Thank you to all of you, who put your personal lives, your feelings, your fears, your good times and bad times out there for people to see. Thank you for not being afraid to show the world, to show us, that there are others out there who know what this life is like. Thank you for sharing the struggles that're small, like the heels that are just too tight, to the struggles that are big, like being misgendered or unaccepted. Thank you for celebrating your triumphs, like that first shot of estrogen or being called ma'am by someone you don't know."

There was a smattering of applause. Megan help up her hand. "Thank you to everyone at Fantasia Fair who have always supported couples like us," she said. "We need people like you to be brave and talk about the struggles and triumphs that we face every day, people who make us understand we're not alone." More applause, and then

Sherry, who'd been dabbing at her eyes, continued. "The Navajo Indians say that a two-spirited person, a person of a feminine nature in a male body, is someone special. Someone sacred." She looked around. "If that's true, then we're surrounded by holiness here, and we just want you to know how much we appreciate it. So now...let's all celebrate!"

We had waitstaff from the restaurant and dining room on hand to pass around the glasses of champagne and plates of finger foods, and Martin had really outdone himself with presenting the oysters; I gave him a thumbs-up.

And then there was a stir by the doorway and Mirela said something but I couldn't make it out, because I was already pushing my way none-too-gently to where Glenn and Mike had just come in.

19

I still couldn't believe my eyes.

We were sitting in Mike's office. He'd produced a bottle of Jameson's from a bottom drawer and he and Glenn and I all drank our own private toast.

What was strange was listening to Mike babble. It must have been from the relief he was feeling, but the flow of words was astonishing. "God," he said feelingly. "I'll never take my own bed for granted again. I'll never take a hot shower for granted again." He glanced at Glenn. "Both of which I hope to become reacquainted with very soon," he said. He took a hefty swallow of whisky. "I've never experienced anything like that before," he told me. "I can't think what it's like—I mean, how anybody survives jail. You lose everything. Someone else controls when you eat, who you see, whether you sleep. It's a nightmare."

"How did you do it?" I asked Glenn.

"I didn't do it. Margaret did it," he said. "All I did was hire her."

"Margaret?"

"Attorney," Mike told me. "The best on the Cape."

I took a quick swallow of Jameson's. I hate Jameson's. I didn't even care. The world seemed to be just a little bit back on track again. "But how?" I asked once the alcohol had finished burning its way down my throat and into my chest. A terrible thought seized me. "Wait. Is this just a bail thing? Are you okay, or is this going to trial?"

"Charges dropped," said Glenn with some satisfaction.

"For now," Mike said.

"For good," said Glenn.

"I don't know," said Mike. "I have a feeling they'd love to reinstate the charges. I seem to be their best option."

"Your hands are too big," I said suddenly.

"I beg your pardon?"

I leaned forward. "Ali called," I said. "He asked his sister–"

"Oh, God, not *that* again," said Glenn. I think he had visions of owing every good thing that happened in his life to the Boston police commissioner.

"Yes, that again," I said. "And the person who killed Angela was shorter than she was, and the person who killed Elizabeth had a small hand span."

Both men tried out their hand spans. Maybe it's an automatic reaction.

Glenn cleared his throat. "In any case," he said, "what Margaret said was that the evidence was circumstantial. And once she had the whole story…"

"Which we don't need to go into right now," said Mike, interrupting. He looked nervous. I've never seen Mike looking nervous. Not like that. "Tell me," I urged. I'm not in Mirela's league, mind you, but even I can detect the potential for good gossip when it hits me over the head.

Mike looked away. Glenn cleared his throat. I got impatient. "Come on, what is it?" I asked. "I'll promise not to tell, if that helps. Cross my heart, hope to die."

"Don't say that," said Glenn quickly.

Mike sighed and poured us each another round. "It's stupid," he began.

"It saved you from a lifetime of being some gang member's best friend," Glenn said to him. "Don't think you'd have liked that."

"Will someone please just *tell* me?" I demanded.

Mike took another fast drink. Glenn looked at him with tolerance and some amusement and said, "Apparently Mike and Adrienne…"

I gasped. "No!"

"Yes," he said, nodding.

"It lasted about half an hour," said Mike. He sounded irritated.

"It lasted a week," Glenn told me.

"You and *Adrienne?*" I said to Mike. Of course, he and Martin were the only people–along with the hapless kitchen crew–who ever got to interact with Adrienne. I only knew her by legend. There had been times when I was pretty sure that she didn't actually exist. Adrienne and Mike?

"For about *five minutes*," he said repressively.

"Let me guess," I said, giggling. "She let you touch her…knives!"

"This is why I didn't want to talk about it," Mike said to Glenn. "My one time with a woman, and it had to be Adrienne. I knew Sydney'd react this way."

"Saved you, though, didn't it?" Glenn asked. He leaned back in his chair, a big, affable bear of a man. I truly wanted to hug him. I resisted the impulse. "Who got him to admit it?"

"Margaret. The lawyer," Glenn said. "She's tough."

"As tough as Adrienne?" Either the Jameson's or the lack of sleep was making me silly.

"Stop it," Mike said sharply. "It was a mistake, all right? It was last week when we were getting ready for Fantasia Fair and we had that unexpected group from Finland and so many people were out with the 'flu and we were all pitching in to help, you remember, well, you were in the thick of it yourself."

Not as much as you were, apparently. "So?"

A big sigh. He really, really didn't like talking about this. "So remember that Martin was out Thursday and Friday last week? I filled in for him."

So much had happened since last week, it felt like a year ago already. But I did remember, vaguely. I'd had two big weddings to conduct so I'd been largely off the hook, personally, but I remembered Mike seemingly everywhere, even helping out with the housekeeping. Glenn cleaning the pool, Brian cleaning rooms, and Mike doing just about everything…"Saturday night, it was impossible," he said. "Huge adrenaline high. Everyone moving at the speed of light to get things done, the dishes prepped and served. Adrienne was screaming at everyone, as she does. One of the busboys said he'd had enough and was going to quit and she went after him with a knife, saying she'd kill him first…I grabbed her and made them both see reason. He stayed, she stayed, and I took the knives. Later when it was all over and I gave them back to her…well, she was feeling more inclined to be rational, and then after that there we were alone in the kitchen and one thing led to another…"

I held up a hand. "Stop there," I said. "I'm too young and innocent to hear any more. And, besides, I eat food that comes out of that kitchen."

"It gets cleaned every day," said Mike with some dignity.

"The point is," said Glenn, "that his fingerprints are on a lot of things that Adrienne–um–has, and they ran them and the knife that ended up in Angela's back had fingerprints, sure, but just a few points of comparison–I think I got that right–so not enough to convict. I don't think they planned to tell us that."

"Points of comparison?" I asked.

"Don't you watch TV?" he asked, irritated. "You need a certain number of points to be sure a fingerprint matches. Margaret says there were some that corresponded with Mike's, but not enough. And there were other prints, but they didn't have enough points to compare to anything."

"Like someone else had handled it?" I asked.

"Like more than one someone else had handled it," he said. "They weren't going to tell us that. Margaret found out."

Whoever this Margaret was, she was formidable. "What about the guest who says she saw you with it?" I asked.

He shrugged. "I don't know what to make of that," he said. "I never had those knives anywhere in a public space. I put them here, in the desk, and seriously only for a couple of hours. I haven't seen them or touched them since then."

Nor, presumably, had he touched Adrienne since then, either. I was dying to know the end of *that* story–it seemed to me somehow that one didn't just walk away from Adrienne, unless she was totally on board with the idea–but it wasn't getting us any further here. "How did your attorney find out?" I asked instead.

Glenn smiled, a slow delighted smile. "Adrienne told her," he said. "Grabbed her by her jacket lapels and pulled her out her chair and wouldn't stop until Margaret did something about it."

Mike said, "I thought Margaret was going to kill her. No one's ever done that to Margaret before, I'll bet."

Now there, I thought, was an image that I wasn't going to forget anytime soon. I was going to have to meet Adrienne. And maybe even Margaret. Someday. "So we're good," I said.

"We're good," said Mike.

"Except that they still don't know who did it," said Glenn.

Mike waved a hand wearily. "It is *so* not my problem anymore," he said. "Sorry, Glenn, I know it reflects on the Race Point Inn and all that, but I'm so *so* not interested in anything right now but a hot shower and another couple of drinks and my own bed." He looked somewhere out beyond exhausted.

Glenn downed the rest of his drink and set it on the desk with finality. "Off you go, then," he said. "The Fair people are great, they'll keep things running, and so will we." A gesture that included me. "Get some rest."

"I might go, too," I said to Glenn, standing up and following them out of the office, hoping that he wouldn't come up with a reason for me to have to stay. Of course, unlike Mike, I didn't have any riveting and impressive *reasons* for being tired, but my insomnia was catching up with me. I had a burning feeling behind my eyes and my limbs all felt like they weighed a ton.

Rachel was hovering near the front desk. "Oh, good, there you are, sweetie!" she said to me, smiling at the two men as they passed by, her hand on my arm to detain me. "What a lovely, lovely ceremony that was!" she exclaimed.

"They're lovely people," I said. I was sincere: I'd learned a lot from Sherry and Megan.

"They are," she said warmly. "And now after dinner you'll get to see my favorite event! Well, honestly, it's *everyone's* favorite event. We do *love* our fashion show. Right now they're practicing for their moment on the catwalk. And, oh, Sydney, it was so *amazing* of you to have a catwalk constructed just for us!"

"That was Mike," I mumbled. "He's the genius. Rachel, this is all a lot of fun, but I'm thinking of giving the fashion show a miss." I paused. "Um–I don't really *do* fashion, in case you hadn't noticed."

"Hmm." She looked me up and down, her eyes assessing. "Well, never mind. You're not going to be *in* the show, just watch it."

"Rachel–"

She reached out and grabbed a passing guest. "Zia, tell Sydney that she absolutely has to come to the fashion show tonight," she said.

The guest was wearing a spectacular blonde wig with lots and lots of blue eye shadow. Dolly Parton, circa 1980. "You should come," she said to me, nodding. "The emcees are funny, the dresses are gorgeous, and we all have a really good time."

"You can't miss it now," said Rachel. "Not after everything you've been through. This is the heart and soul of Fantasia Fair. It's an excuse to just relax. Have a few laughs. Play with glamour. Be like everybody else."

I sighed. "You're going to say yes," said Rachel, nodding encouragingly.

"Yeah," I said. "I'm going to say yes."

Oh, goodie.

20

The fashion show, as it turned out, was a cross between Hollywood in the 1940s and Las Vegas in the present…glitz and glamour topped with a good-sized helping of nostalgia.

I was sitting near the back and watching the audience almost as much as the emcees. Rachel had been right: there was such a sense of relaxation in the room, an air of lightness and fun, all things I suspected was missing in a lot of these guests' lives. Oddly enough, this angered me more than anything else I'd heard or read over the past six months: everyone had a right to nights like this. It was the world that wanted to take it away from people that was sick, not the other way around.

One step into the future. One step at a time.

Glenn was sitting up front at one of the VIP tables with a couple of his bear friends, cocktails in hand, obviously enjoying himself. I found myself thinking about his partner, Barry, and how he'd have loved this, too. Nice men. There were still good people out there. The world wasn't all cruelty.

I waved off the server–if I drank any alcohol, I was going to pass out, I was so tired– and settled in to observe and enjoy. Rachel was right: it was *fun*. There were a few in-jokes that sailed right over my head, but enough of it was inclusive of anybody's experience to be funny. And the fashions…all I could think of was being a little girl and going through my grandmother's clothing after she died, my mother throwing things in a box for the Salvation Army without even looking at them. "I can't believe she wore that!" she snapped, over and over again, and the box filled with boas and lace and glittery camisoles and feathered hats. And I fell in love with all of them. My grandmother, it seemed, had dressed in a style somewhere between Isadora Duncan and Stevie Nicks, and I was enchanted. Later, when the boxes were consigned to the attic–because my mother's efficiency never quite reached as far as actually bringing said boxes to the thrift shop–I crept up and tried everything on. There were fans. There were parasols. And there was an alternate Sydney Riley living in that attic and liking this woman I'd never really known, not least of all because my mother clearly *hadn't* liked her.

Have I mentioned that I have one or two very tiny mother issues?

Gradually I became aware of Rachel standing in the doorway. No clipboard, tonight, and dressed down, in a trouser suit and flat shoes. Checking her watch. Once an organizer, always an organizer, I thought, feeling an odd connection to her: even in the middle of one thing, she was probably going through lists and arrangements in her head. It's what I did, when I had an event going.

And then the door opened and Gertie, the new front-desk clerk, passed Rachel a note. Rachel held the door slightly open with her foot while she used the ambient light to read the note, and then she looked up from it, around the room, and–to my surprise–slipped out the door.

I was out of my seat before I even had time to think about it. It was that look, that furtiveness, that made me decide before I consciously decided anything. If there was something going on, I needed to know about it. Professionally.

And personally. Let's face it, I'm as much a snoop as Mirela.

At the reception desk, Gertie was just saying to Rachel, "…and all I know is, Brian said you should get it at 8:30." She caught sight of me over Rachel's shoulder and smiled in relief. "Sydney can probably straighten it out," she said.

"I doubt that," said Rachel, sounding most un-Rachel-like. Cold.

"Are you all right?" I asked her.

"I'm fine. And it's really none of your…" She caught herself, smiled. "Sorry, Sydney. That was uncalled for. Just a lot on my mind. You should go back in, you're missing the show."

"So are you," I pointed out. "Maybe I can help. If there's something wrong, Rachel—"

She glanced at Gertie, and shook her head. "Nothing's wrong," she said. "Just need a breath of fresh air, that's all. I'll take a quick walk, clear my head. I'll be right back." And she had turned away before I could respond.

I watched her go through the front door. This wasn't right; there was something else going on. She could have had it flash in big neon lights over her head and it might have been ever-so-slightly more obvious. This was one of her really big nights, and she needed to take a walk in the middle of it?

She'd been about to say it was none of my business, and she was probably right. That's okay: something being none of my business has never stopped me before. I headed out after her. "Rachel, wait!"

She turned, standing under the streetlamp outside the inn. There was moisture in the air, a slight mist, and she looked like she was on stage, spotlighted. Almost a halo. "What *is* it, Sydney?"

"I can help," I said. "Really. If–"

"No." She cut me off quickly. "Listen, just leave me alone, okay? I have something to do, and then I'll be back." There was something in her voice, a hint of excitement coursing through her words. Anticipation, but not in a good way. Around us, outside the pool of light, the night suddenly felt very dark, the street deserted.

"You're not coming back," I said slowly. "What's going on, Rachel? Is it about Angela and Elizabeth?"

She looked at me sharply. "No."

But it was; I knew it. And I was suddenly seeing a film unwind, scenes following each other like a speeded-up video. Rachel's reaction when she found out Angela was a cop, the look of what had to be fear on her face. I'd thought she was afraid for Angela, for her sake, for the way the other cops would have treated her. What had Rachel done to make her scared of a cop?

Rachel hurrying to surround Angela with other guests, and Taisie's voice: "That's not like her, usually she's the one to go around asking people for help, introducing her around." And Megan: "We'll make up for it, but it's weird, isn't it?"

And Rachel: "I used to live in Trenton. The armpit of the universe. We had a mutually agreed-upon breakup, that city and me."

I was staring at her now. Was my whole theory about the murder wrong? Maybe it wasn't Coral who was the intended victim; maybe it had been Angela, all along. Had she recognized Rachel from the past? Was there something that Rachel had to fear from her?

Could Rachel have *killed* her?

Rachel said, calmly, "I don't know what you're thinking, Sydney, but whatever it is, it's wrong. Go back to the fashion show. This doesn't concern you."

"Convince me."

An exaggerated sigh. "I don't think I need to convince *you* of anything. Frankly, this isn't your business. This is something personal."

I moistened my lips. I was scared. I remembered what had happened here at the inn last year; my first (and only, I'd fervently hoped) encounter with a murderer. Knowing a person who was willing to kill, and never having guessed who it was. Was Rachel one of them? *Could* she have done it? I liked her–actually, I liked her a lot. She was smart and self-deprecating and funny. I'd been looking forward to becoming friends. I didn't–I couldn't–see her as a criminal on the lam. I couldn't see her knifing one person and strangling another and staying so calm and possessed about it. This had to be something else. It had to be. "Tell me you didn't run away from the cops in New Jersey," I said. "Tell me it wasn't that Angela scared you."

She stood there for a moment, the sequins on her jacket glittering under the streetlight, looking at me. A stray wind funneled up Commercial Street and lifted her hair. "All right," she said at last. "If it will get you off my back...I'd met Angela before. As Bob. Who knew, huh?" She was trying to sound rueful. "Small world. Ridiculously small world. And he knew me, too...as Roger." She took a breath. "So now you have it. That's all there is to it. It's not a time in my life I'm really proud of, and it was a long time ago. What's the expression—it was in another country, and besides, the wench is dead? I'd all but forgotten it."

"What did you do? Why were you in trouble with the cops?"

"Nothing impressive," she said, turning up her collar; she'd felt that wind, too. "Certainly nothing that would make me want to kill him."

"I don't pretend to understand what makes people want to kill other people," I said. "But you have to admit, it's suspicious."

"Oh, for heaven's sake!" she exclaimed, impatient. "I still don't see how it's your business, but...It was seventeen years ago. I was in my early twenties. I'd been completely rejected by my family. They turned me out, disowned me, the whole drama. I'd lost my job. In case you hadn't noticed...we're vulnerable, when we're alone and dealing with how people see us."

"I get that," I said. I was starting to feel seriously chilly and wished she'd just get on with it. "Don't play the victim card here, Rachel."

"I'm not. I'm not a victim now, and I wasn't a victim then. I just did what I had to do to survive. I took things into my own hands. I did some shoplifting. I sold some drugs. I did what I had to do, and I survived things you've never even dreamed of in your protected little world, and I came out on the other side. Actually, in more than one way." She allowed herself a smile. "I'm someone now. I've become successful. I'm Rachel; Roger is gone, dead, part of someone else's past."

"Let me guess," I said. "You thought there might still be open warrants. That Angela might take you back to New Jersey." That was patently ridiculous: Angela had other, far more important things on her mind. Surely Rachel would have seen that.

She lifted her shoulders. "Who knows? All I knew is that I wanted to keep my distance from–Angela." A pause. "But I didn't kill her, Sydney."

"I want to believe you," I said. And I did; I really did. I liked Rachel. I didn't want her to be a bad person. I took a deep internal breath. *Use your brain, Riley.* Rachel was taller than Angela, her hands were male-large. It couldn't have been her.

So what was she doing slipping furtively out into the October night?

She tossed her head. "Then believe me, or don't believe me," she said impatiently. "I don't care. It's all fine with me. I'm not going to stand here and try to convince you. And unless you're going to make a citizen's arrest here, I'm going for my walk."

"To meet whoever left you that note?"

"To think some things out. Things that pertain to the note, yeah. But that's all. And it's personal, none of your—"

"—business. I know," I finished for her. She was right, and I was feeling slightly ridiculous standing there, all my confused thoughts coalescing slowly and making no sense at all. I had no idea what the hell was going on, but I wasn't getting anywhere standing here giving her stern looks. "Okay, Rachel." I turned back toward the inn. "Good luck—if you're in a position to need it."

"I'll see you later," she said firmly.

"Yeah. Okay." I went up the steps and sensed rather than saw her turn away and head up Commercial Street toward the center of town. I took a deep breath, walked through reception and kept going out the side door, over to where we kept the bike rack. With spare bikes for the guests. Blessedly unlocked.

Whatever it was that Rachel had to hide, I was determined that I was going to find out about it.

***

She wasn't hard to follow. There were a few people around, looking into the lighted windows of the hat shop and a couple of the galleries, pulling scarves and jackets closer around them, taking one last after-dinner stroll before heading back to the bed-and-breakfast. My bicycle's tires were silent, far quieter than my footsteps would have been; I glided in and out of pools of brightness from streetlight to streetlight, matching Rachel's brisk pace. She knew where she was going, and I wasn't altogether surprised when she entered Lopes Square and headed down the pier.

Above us, the Pilgrim Monument was lit up, a ghostly white tower piercing the darkness, stars winking around it, diamonds on velvet. Someone was probably out taking a photo of it. Someone was always out taking a photo of it.

The pier was much better lit than the streets, and I hung back a little. It was deserted, and the wind—with no buildings to cut it—whipped cold and strong. No one was around: the ferries don't run at night, and all the fishing fleet–such as it is–seemed to be in.

Rachel didn't hesitate: she went all the way to the end, walking briskly, and I followed, coasting, slowly and silently.

I veered over to the right finally and tucked my bicycle in on the side of the pirate museum, creeping around to the front, hoping that I would be hidden in its shadows. I was going to have to work on my ninja technique.

Across from us, on Fisherman's Wharf, the large-scale portraits of the Portuguese grandmothers on the side of the wharf building looked askance at us. As well they might, I thought. Though there's nothing much that Portuguese grandmothers haven't faced, in their time.

Rachel was standing near the harbormaster's office, now closed and darkened; they don't maintain a 24-hour presence on the pier. The harsh lighting from standards a hundred feet up reduced her to something black and white, a stick figure, a caricature. A small figure on a stage. Behind her, the fishing boats moved gently against each other. "I'm here!" she called out, finally, turning around so that she could look all over the area.

No response.

Rachel waited, then tried again. "I don't know what this note's about," she called, her voice absorbed into the sound of the water lapping at the pilings beneath us. Over my head, a gull suddenly screamed, and I jumped. The darkness seemed to be moving closer. "I thought our arrangements were clear!"

"Not clear enough," said Taisie Murray, stepping out from the shadows behind the harbormaster building. "Not even close to clear enough."

Taisie?

Rachel seemed to relax when she saw Taisie, her shoulders slumping slightly. Now at least she knew where to look, whom to address. "You said it's an emergency," she said, her voice level. "It had better be. I'm not accustomed to missing the fashion show."

"Oh, my God. You and your fashion show," Taisie said. "All of you, your precious show, and your precious clothes. We're only three days in, and I'm completely sick of it already. You know that Peter owns more dresses than I do?"

"Coral," Rachel said calmly. "*Coral* owns more dresses than you do."

"Stupid name," said Taisie. "Stupid name, stupid clothes, and such incredible stupidity to come to this idiotic fair, year after year, feel great about hanging out with other men who like to dress as women and then still want to have sex with women." She peered at Rachel. "Except for you, of course."

"Except for me?" Her voice was still steady, but Rachel had looked around her, quickly, nervous for the first time, looking for—what? A weapon? A place to hide?

Something here wasn't right.

"At least you're realistic. At least you don't pretend that having a penis and having a dress are compatible." There was more than scorn in her voice; there was venom. Hidden in my shadows, I shivered. I wouldn't want that voice directed at me. "At least you know that you were supposed to be a woman. At least you're trying to fix things."

Rachel didn't rise to it. "Taisie, why am I here?"

"*Rachel*," she said, mimicking Rachel's voice, "you seem to think that you're still in control here. I find that interesting, and not very smart. You really think I'd call you out to a deserted place like this just to pass the time of day?"

And then I saw it, glinting in the hard lighting, the flash of something in her hand. *No*, I thought: *no, no, no…*

Rachel hadn't seen it, or if she had, she didn't believe Taisie was really going to do anything with it. "We've got an arrangement. That's all there is to talk about. And if there's nothing else, I'm going back to the show now. I suggest you do the same, and…"

It happened quickly, before I had time to react, before Rachel had time to react: the three quick steps, the thrust in and up, and Rachel's hands suddenly clutching the hilt of the knife buried in her abdomen. I was screaming and running toward them without thinking about what I was doing, an automatic reaction, just wanting to do something, down on my knees next to Rachel as she fell slowly–television apparently got that detail right–and grabbing and holding her against me. "Rachel!"

Her eyes were glassy. I couldn't tell if she was breathing or not. I looked up. "Call 911!" I gasped, not even registering how ridiculous it was to ask Taisie for help. "We have to get an ambulance."

If she'd been shocked to see me, she'd gotten over it quickly. She was silhouetted against the light; I couldn't see her face, just shadows. Darkness. Creepy. "Taisie, *help*!"

"You know," she said slowly, as though considering it, "I really think not."

I bent back down over Rachel, listening for breathing. Could you perform CPR on someone who'd been stabbed? I had no idea. I was willing to give it a try–

And then there were amazingly strong hands lifting me up and backward, and Taisie—who was actually pretty tall for a cis woman, taller than me—was behind me, her forearm my neck. *Holy shit. She wants to kill me.*

There was a roaring in my ears. I wiggled, my hands up on top of her arm, trying to move it, it wasn't working, and panic setting in *I can't breathe I can't breathe I can't breathe…*

Taisie was grunting with the effort, pulling me backward, and it was starting to be clear I wasn't going to dislodge her. I didn't feel strong enough to keep trying. Everything was getting horribly dark around the edges and I was going to have to do something but if I stomped on her foot or something it might make her really, really angry and…

The woman's already trying to kill you, Riley. Exactly how is making her angry going to make things any worse?

I brought my heel down, hard, on her foot, my elbow into her gut, everything getting automatic because that blackness was moving in toward the center and some detached part of me was already thinking, okay, now I know how I'm dying, when she swore sharply with the pain and let up. I staggered forward, gasping and heaving, and I could feel rather than see her coming at me again, making an odd sound that I couldn't interpret and I knew I couldn't do this again, so I did the only thing I could think of doing.

I ran, and jumped off the pier.

21

I only had impressions, after that. The water was cold enough to shock me, it was painful, cold that hurt, and I couldn't swim, my limbs felt like jelly, the cold and the pain were just too much. *Ironic*, I thought, *if I get away from a killer to just die here in the harbor.*

Like Dorothy Bradford. The wife of the future first governor of Massachusetts had endured the months at sea on the Mayflower, through wind and storms and the perilous crossing of the dangerous North Atlantic, and then, once the ship was safely in harbor, on a bright sunny day, she slipped off the deck, fell into the harbor, and drowned. Did she jump, or was she pushed? The question suddenly seemed immensely important to me. "Dorothy," I gasped, and I wondered if I'd see her swimming beside me when I drowned, going down into the black water for the last time. Maybe she was here now. Maybe...

And then someone was pulling me up and out, and a voice was saying, "Sydney. Hold onto me, damn it. Sydney!"

"Dorothy!" I gasped again, and a man's voice said, "oh, for God's sake," and pulled me roughly over the gunwale and into a boat.

The stench of fish was overwhelming, and I threw up then, all over the boat, all over my rescuer, who I could finally identify as Mike. "Oh, fucking A!" he exclaimed, pushing me off him.

"Am I alive?" I couldn't quite believe it.

"Not much longer, if you keep up stunts like that," he complained. "I might get violent myself. This coat was *clean*."

"Not anymore," I said, and started giggling. And couldn't stop.

***

A lot happened after that, most of which was a little hazy for me. Someone wrapped me in a blanket and said something about hypothermia. Someone else handed me something hot to drink.

In the meantime, the police and rescue squad were both busy. Rachel–who was, somehow, amazingly still alive–was stabilized and medevac'd to a trauma center in Boston. Taisie, who'd had time to get her car and take off, was pulled over before she even got to the Truro line. It's hard to escape from Cape Cod: there's only one road out of town. Any town.

And when Ali found out, having been alerted by Glenn, he managed to somehow get helicoptered in. It was never clear to me if it was via homeland security or ICE or the Boston police. Perhaps just as well. A couple of EMTs pronounced that I would live, and someone took me back to the inn where I got to stand under a hot shower for twenty minutes and get wrapped in one of the fluffy white robes from the spa. The state police wanted to talk to me. Julie wanted to talk to me.

I wanted to find out how Mike, last seen trudging off home after enduring a night in the cellblock, had just happened to be floating along under the pier at just the right moment.

I was sitting in the parlor on a love seat, Ali beside me, my hands wrapped around a mug that contained tea and brandy. It tasted awful. I had some beautiful bruising coming up nicely on my neck. But everything was well: I was alive, I was slowly getting warm, my boyfriend was sitting next to me; and in that moment, that was heaven enough.

Mike was drinking something, too; I hoped that it tasted better than my concoction. "So what happened," he said, going over what he'd already explained to the state police, "is that I got home and I was all set to just relax, but something was bothering me. Remember how me and Glenn, we got to the patio right at the end of your wedding ceremony?"

"It was a renewal of vows," I said. I had no idea why I needed to get that right.

"Rachel was near me, talking on her mobile. She didn't see me, she was behind that awful viburnum thing you have out there."

"It isn't awful," I protested.

"What was she saying?" asked Ali.

"I didn't know who she was talking to, and I wasn't really listening, you know, just glad to be back, feeling relieved, but I guess I heard it without paying attention and it came back to me later. She said that the other person, the person she was talking to, was safe as long as the money was delivered on time. Well, that could be nothing, right? I mean, Sydney's always talking about deliveries, and Rachel was an event coordinator too."

"Is," I said. "She *is* an event coordinator."

"Right," said Mike. "But that business about delivering money—that was just jarring, you know? And the more I tried not to think about it, the more it stuck. I took a shower and had something to eat, but I couldn't stop thinking about it, and...hell, I don't know, Sydney. It was just a feeling that something was terribly wrong."

"Thank God for that feeling," said Ali. I nodded and took another swallow of the horrible potion they'd given me. It was working; I was finally feeling warm inside, too.

"So I came back to the inn," said Mike. "Feeling just a little stupid. The fashion show was going on, people laughing and applauding, you'd never believe anything was wrong. But as soon as I got there Gertie told me that someone had given Brian a note for Gertie to deliver to Rachel Parsons at exactly eight-thirty, and that she'd done it, and that Rachel and Sydney had had some words, and that you'd both left then. And about then Coral came around, asking if we'd seen Taisie, saying that Taisie had disappeared and she was worried. That Taisie had seemed—off, some-how." He shook his head. "It felt like the whole evening was going wrong in some in-definable way. Like, I don't know, Mercury retrograde or something."

But Coral added that Taisie had said she was going out to the pier, and so Mike thought he'd just take a look, see what was what, just to assuage his conscience. And the most discreet way he'd known how to do it was to take his flatbed oystering dinghy out, paddling silently on the black water, a few oysters from what he'd collected for the party's raw bar still on the boat's bottom. "As soon as I saw you go in, I moved fast. I knew you didn't have long," he said. "Water's 50 degrees. Of course, I didn't know you were half unconscious already."

"Thanks, Mike," I said. The words were inadequate as hell. How do you thank some-one for saving your life? I took a deep breath. "So what do we know? Who knows what's going on?"

Ali knew. That fraternity of law enforce-ment again. "Taisie's made a statement," he said. "She's wanted out of her marriage for a while—apparently Peter's transformation into Coral wasn't as welcome to her as she'd let on. But she didn't want to go through a di-vorce, she thought that would be uncool somehow, people would see her as bigoted or something."

"Heaven forbid," I said, and, "she *was* bigoted," Glenn said at the same time.

"Some bigots don't self-define that way," said Ali smoothly. He should know: he's had more than a little experience with hate crimes himself. "Anyway, at the end of the day, she wanted him dead for the oldest of reasons: the money. She took out two life insurance policies. Together they're almost eight hundred thousand dollars. It was that simple."

"And she didn't know that Angela was wearing Coral's dress," I said. "See? I was right, after all! It was a case of mistaken identity." I paused. "Wow, what a panic. Imagine how she must have felt when she realized she'd killed the wrong person."

"Determined to get it right the next time," Ali said. "She wasn't going to give up just because she'd screwed up. She didn't panic. She thought it all through, and she recovered with a contingency plan." He rubbed my neck. "She was in it for the money, just like 80 or so percent of the murders out there. That's one way this community isn't all that different from any other. People will always kill each other for gain."

"That's bleak," said Glenn.

"That's reality," Ali said. "And it didn't particularly bother her that she'd killed the wrong person."

Glenn nodded. "Turns out she left a note at the desk," he said.

"There's what I was looking for! Her modus operandi," I said. "She left notes. And that's great evidence, too, isn't it?"

Glenn took a drink. "She told Brian to give it to the woman in the red dress and shoes," he said. "He didn't read it, and it's gone now, but it probably said to meet her on the beach. And Angela, who wanted to belong so desperately, went to see what was up. Maybe she thought it was someone befriending her."

Ali nodded. "So she killed the wrong person," he said again. "But she thought, there's still time to make it right. Hell, if she could keep it up, everyone might even assume they *were* hate crimes, after all."

"And see Provincetown as unsafe," said Mike. He was looking really pale.

"So why go for Elizabeth, then?" I asked. "That doesn't make sense."

"I only got a summary of the preliminary report," said Ali. "She didn't say, or they didn't tell me. But Elizabeth—well, nobody noticed her, did they? She was quiet and scared and who knows what she might have seen or heard? Or what Taisie may have *thought* she'd seen or heard. That would have been enough. So somehow Elizabeth had to go, too." He shrugged. "And then, after that, she still was going to go after Coral," he said. "It's only Wednesday: she had the rest of the week."

Hard to believe it was only Wednesday. One of the longest weeks of my life, so far.

"And Rachel?" asked Mike. "What happened with Rachel?"

I moved restlessly. I wasn't going to like this part. "She said they had an arrangement," I said uncomfortably.

"They did," Ali confirmed. "Rachel found out. Who knows how—you event coordinators, you seem to be everywhere at once. She found out somehow about either Angela, or Elizabeth, or both, and they had a conversation. She probably even *helped* Taisie, by planting that glass with Mike's fingerprints on it next to Elizabeth. Rachel's were on it, too. And Taisie's."

"No one told me that," said Mike.

"Rachel had a lot on Taisie," said Ali.

I *really* wasn't going to like this part. I truly, wholeheartedly liked Rachel. "Let's just call it what it is," I said bleakly. "She was blackmailing Taisie. That's bad enough. But it gets worse. Think about it—the only way that

Taisie was going to be able to pay blackmail was if she got that insurance settlement. And the only way she was getting the insurance settlement was by killing Coral." I took a deep breath. "So Rachel knew that was going to happen, and she wasn't going to tell anyone. She was going to just let Taisie do it. She was going to let it happen."

"People," said Ali after a pause, "are complicated." There was a moment of silence. I didn't want people to be complicated. I wanted them to be clear. Just nice, or just mean. Good guys, or bad guys. "And Rachel needed serious money," he said. "She wanted the operation—the whole gender reassignment thing."

"That's why Taisie said something about Rachel wanting to be a real woman," I said, remembering. "She said something about Rachel at least understanding that she wasn't a real woman and doing something about it."

Ali nodded. "And it's not cheap. But Taisie was going to have plenty of money."

I sighed. "Is she going to make it?" I asked.

"Rachel? Still touch and go," Ali said.

"I think I need to talk to you," I said to Glenn.

***

The next morning I was standing by the front desk when people came down for breakfast. I had a scarf tucked artistically around my neck. I had a clipboard in my hand. "This way," I told the guests, my bright events smile on. "I'm sorry, Rachel Parsons had an accident last night. She's in the hospital."

Murmuring, questions, expressions of sympathy. "What about the rest of the Fair?" someone asked.

I smiled. "No problem," I assured them. "I'm taking it from here."

The End

Twilight People Prayer

As the sun sinks and the colors of the day turn, we offer a blessing for the twilight, for twilight is neither day nor night, but in-between.

We are all twilight people.
We can never be fully labeled or defined.
We are many identities and loves, many genders and none.
We are in between roles, at the intersection of histories, or between place and place.
We are crisscrossed paths of memory and destination, streaks of light swirled together.
We are neither day nor night. We are both, neither, and all.

May the sacred in-between of this evening suspend our certainties, soften our judgments, and widen our vision.
May this in-between light illuminate our way to the God who transcends all categories and definitions.
May the in-between people who have come to pray be lifted up into this twilight.
We cannot always define; we can always say a blessing.
Blessed are You, God of all, who brings on the twilight.

– Rabbi Reuben Zellman, TransTorah.org

Acknowledgments

A tremendous thank you to everyone in the trans community for all the information that they've generously given me over the past year, and especially to Robyn and Audri Bazlen-Weglarz, for whom no question about the Fair was too elementary or too idiotic. Thanks also to Gigi Gorgeous, Deidre Smith, and Ziva Cohen, for opening up the world at large still further. Several additional people who spoke to me wished to remain anonymous; I respect that while waiting for a world in which they don't need to stay hidden.

Special thanks to my beta readers, Margo Nash, Fred Biddle, and Assaf Levavy, for suggestions and for catching so many problems! Margo in particular (my own vision of the Best Lawyer On Cape Cod) was instrumental in turning the modus operandi around and catching both legal and forensic errors. Thanks to my editor, Lynn Benton, for catching–I hope–the rest of the book's mistakes. Dianne Kopser (who really does perform weddings in P'town) always lends a sympathetic ear. Michelle Crone and Deb Karacozian were the first to tell me to write a Provincetown series, which I ignored for far too long. And Beckett kindly allowed me to base the fictional Ibsen on him.

Thanks to Rabbi Reuben Zellman for allowing me to reprint his lovely meditation. TransTorah collects trans and genderqueer Jewish resources to make them accessible to everyone at transtorah.org. And, again, to Meredith Kurkjian Lobur for police stuff.

As always, I am both proud and humbled to work with Arthur Mahoney of Homeport Press, his vision of an organization that supports the written word at land's end; more about them at HomeportPress.com. Miladinka Milic is my inspired and extremely patient cover designer (you can catch her at 99Designs.com). Thanks to my web guy in Ukraine, Kyre Song, who helps me keep a reasonably updated presence online at JeannettedeBeauvoir.com; he's at KyreSong.com. And my writing partner, Assaf Levavy of Israel and Italy, keeps me moving forward. As you can see, my network is international and very, very talented.

Thanks to you all.

Finally, one very special person has read this entire book looking for his name; I can be, however, if not a bear of very little brain then one who loses slips of paper. You know who you are and if you'll contact me at my email address, I'll give your name to three people so it doesn't get lost again and include it in the next book in the series!

Did You Enjoy This Book?

If you did…

1) please share your opinion on Goodreads, Amazon, BN.com, and Powell's.

2) visit my Amazon page and read some of my other books.

3) give the book a boost on by telling people about it on Facebook and Twitter.

4) subscribe to The Novelist's Notebook at www.JeannettedeBeauvoir.com (scroll to bottom of page) for book reviews, short stories, quizzes, free stuff, previews of upcoming work, and more.

5) ask your local bookseller to stock *Murder at Fantasia Fair*

6) make it your choice for your next book-club meeting (I'll even join you by Skype or Zoom if you'd like me to!)

7) email me at JeannettedeBeauvoir@gmail.com and tell me so!

8) And watch for the next in the P'town Theme Week series from Homeport Press!

Made in the USA
Columbia, SC
01 November 2017